SHOW THE COLORS

**Center Point
Large Print**

**This Large Print Book carries the
Seal of Approval of N.A.V.H.**

SHOW THE COLORS

Luke Short, Jr.

CENTER POINT PUBLISHING
THORNDIKE, MAINE

This Center Point Large Print edition
is published in the year 2008 by arrangement with
Daniel Glidden.

The text of this Large Print edition is unabridged. In other
aspects, this book may vary from the original edition.
Printed in the United States of America.
Set in 16-point Times New Roman type.

ISBN: 978-1-60285-174-0

Library of Congress Cataloging-in-Publication Data

Short, Luke.
    Show the colors / Luke Short, Jr.--Center Point large print ed.
        p. cm.
    ISBN 978-1-60285-174-0 (lib. bdg. : alk. paper)
        1. Large type books. I. Title.

PS3569.H59S47 2008
813'.54--dc22

2007051255

CHAPTER
1

Sergeant James "Breed" Stalwart led his detail through the stout log gates of Fort Manning shortly after sunup. The soft, golden-maize light warmed the soldiers. The men cautiously descended the sage-studded plateau on a deeply rutted road that cut through rolling arroyos and parched dry washes before it leveled out in the lush, emerald-green river bottom. The Indian scout No-Feet was ahead, but within earshot. He checked side trails and the skirting hills for signs of marauding Indians. Breed's top soldiers, Troopers Stills and Williams, flanked the immediate ridges to protect two wood-and-water wagons. The "Confederate Connection," three rebel soldiers, Glade, Loppitt, and Bancroft, comprised the bobtailed rearguard. These young men were with General Lee at Appomattox. They were tight.

Breed spurred his mount forward alongside Stills. Together they dropped into a narrow, steep-walled gully. "What do you think, Dave?" Breed questioned the seasoned soldier.

Stills's eyes never stopped searching the encircling hills. "They're here," Dave cautioned Breed, "and we've blundered into it. What are we doing with this collection of malcontents and misfits? We would be better off alone." Dave pulled at the corner of his bushy mustache.

"These are the best I could find." Breed smiled sadly.

Stills laughed. "Williams will get a crookneck from watchin' his backside." The trooper shook his head in disbelief. "At least our forward flanks are safe."

"Stay ready, Dave," Breed warned him. "Let's not get caught out here."

They angled across the slope and continued to scour the hillside. As they crested the ridge No-Feet slowly returned to the troopers. He was turned halfway on his pony, rifle braced against his thigh. Instantly Breed sensed the detail was in trouble.

Fort Manning was critically short of personnel, which left it in a dangerous and vulnerable predicament. The commanding officer, General Shenandoah Clemments, along with two full cavalry companies, was on a grueling month-long campaign against the Apaches. In the southwest corner of the Arizona Territory, bordering Chihuahua, Mexico, Mexican bandits and Apaches were fighting together to isolate and destroy the string of U.S. Army forts that paralleled the border. Fort Washburn had been abandoned—a tactical retreat, in military jargon. The Indians burned it to the ground.

General Clemments led a reinforced supply patrol to Fort Bennet, which had suffered under a prolonged siege. This mission had become a deadly game of ambush and surprise attacks. The Mexicans operated with a free hand out of Mexico and constantly harassed the soldiers. The troopers held their own, but counterattacks were futile, as the Mexicans fled across the border into the Sierra Madres. The Apaches took advantage of time and terrain to ambush the pony soldiers at will.

Breed knew they were in for a fight. He spurred his horses forward to meet No-Feet. Stills followed close behind. Suddenly two Apaches appeared approximately seventy yards in front of them. Both were mounted on sturdy ponies. They baited the soldiers in hopes of a chase. One of the Indians smacked his buttock contemptuously with an open hand.

"How many are there, No-Feet?"

The Apache answered Breed's question while watching the Indians. "Ten riders in that deep arroyo and tracks of twelve behind the bluff." He pinpointed the spot. "Maybe six near the river bottom."

Breed thought, Thirty against eleven. Damn, they're cocky. Spoilin' for a fight. He spoke. "We don't stand a chance, Dave. Head for the wagons. Turn them around and be ready for a wild dash to the fort."

Dave Stills gently nudged his horse down the gradual slope to the wagons. Breed watched him talk with the drivers, Sergeant Fitz and Private Hinton. Stills helped the slow-witted private turn his wagon. The teams walked slowly toward the fort. Each wagon had an armed soldier in the back.

"When you're ready, we go," Breed told the scout.

As he spoke, six Indians joined the pair already on the road. Breed felt a twinge of apprehension when he saw their leader, Walking Tall. Here was a cunning adversary. Breed had fought him in the past, and respected him.

Walking Tall and his braves were dressed in long-sleeved shirts, long pants of heavy handwoven cloth, and knee-length leather moccasins. The Indian chief wore a dark brown leather vest that accentuated his big frame. His handsome chiseled facial features were framed by thick black hair tied back with a red head-band. The man cast an imposing shadow. Breed chuckled to himself. A big man like that makes a fine target. Slowly Breed pulled his rifle from the scabbard and laid it across his lap. He counted three rifles among the eight Indians. Three were armed with bows and two carried lances.

The Indians bunched together. Waiting for what? Breed pondered. Abruptly No-Feet glanced past Breed's shoulder to the bluff. A faint spiral of dust drifted skyward behind it. Surrounded. No-Feet and Breed wheeled their horses and whipped them in a desperate run for the fort. Breed hollered frantically at Williams and Stills to ride to the nearby low ridge of the bluff. They realized what was happening and urged their mounts forward, knowing the ridge to be their only salvation. Sergeant Fitz and Private Hinton savagely cracked the reins over their teams, trying to milk the last ounce of strength and speed from the horses.

The death race was on. Breed and No-Feet quickly caught the lumbering wagons which were throwing billowing, choking clouds of dust. As Breed and No-Feet passed the wagons, they watched the three-man Confederate rearguard gallop up the steep hill of the plateau and reach safety. Breed snapped a quick glance at the ridgeline and watched as Stills and Williams leapt from their mounts. They sprinted the last remaining feet to the ridge and belly-flopped down. Seconds later they were shooting at the encircling Indians. Breed turned to No-Feet. "We made it," he shouted excitedly.

Breed and No-Feet galloped three quarters of the distance up the road to a shallow wash. Quickly they dismounted, ran to the side, and used it as a breastwork. The wagon teams, lathered and winded, strained on the final pull. The Indians gained steadily. Neither rifleman in the wagons had yet fired a shot. As the wagons closed on them, Breed heard shots and war cries within the dust cloud. He thumbed back the hammer of his rifle, sighted off to one side of the wagons, and fired blindly into the brown wall of dust. No-Feet did the same.

They quickly reloaded and waited for a target. When the rear wagon thundered past, Breed caught the blurred outline of an Indian, and snapped off a quick shot. He saw the pony go down but wasn't convinced he had hit the brave. No-Feet singled out a charging Indian and shot at him. A second pony went down whinnying in terror and pain.

The dust cloud thinned and settled. Breed could see the Indians slowly withdrawing. Two were doubled up. One of the ponies thrashed wildly and staggered to its feet. The pony's front leg dangled uselessly. Breed put the sight bead slightly in back of the animal's shoulder and squeezed off the shot. The pony dropped and stayed down. Walking Tall and his braves arrogantly rode on the road which they owned at the moment.

The volume of fire coming from Stills and Williams caught Breed's attention. Badly outgunned, the two soldiers were being forced from the ridge. Breed and No-Feet would provide covering fire. Breed whistled at Stills but Dave did not hear him. Breed hollered at the top of his lungs. No response. Desperately Breed fired below and to the right of Stills. The trooper jerked around, fearing entrapment. Breed whistled and motioned them to fall back. Dave nudged Williams; together they sprinted to their horses, mounted, and raced for the road. Breed concentrated on the ridgeline and watched for movement. He spotted a blur beside a small rock on the skyline, drew a bead on the rock, and shot. No more movement. A quivering sage bush elicited the same response from No-Feet. The heavy slug exploded through the ridge. Only a foolhardy Indian would venture over the top.

The two troopers pounded past Breed and No-Feet and rode to the breakover of the plateau. They dismounted and immediately took firing positions. Stills and Williams peppered the ridge while Breed and No-Feet withdrew. Not a shot was fired at them.

"Thanks, you guys," Breed offered as he rode onto the plateau. "That was mighty close." He relied once again on these two veteran fighters.

"I know I said it before, Breed." Stills laughed. "What a bunch of misfits." Breed couldn't keep a straight face. Williams chewed on his toothpick and merely shook his head in disbelief.

"Those are some of the U.S. Army's finest," Breed told Dave. Stills held out his hands and pantomimed a bad case of the tremors.

The three hardened soldiers shared the moment, a soldier's camaraderie bonding them. Breed's quick sense of humor and easygoing nature made him likable. He was consistently even-tempered. His men knew what was expected of them, and acted accordingly. He asked nothing of them that he would not do himself. These qualities attracted men like Stills and Williams.

Breed had grown up hard. Tough challenges were continually hurled at him. He was the runt of three brothers, and everything he'd gotten he'd scrapped and fought for. While his father and brothers were fair, they'd pushed him constantly. He had matured into a strapping one-hundred-and-eighty-pound man, a tad shy of six feet. Long, unkempt curly black hair covered his collar. His rugged, sun-weathered face was deeply lined. Breed's eyes, set and piercing, had a barely detectable gentle quality to them.

Breed's father's untimely death by drowning had thrown chaos into the tightly knit family. Then the Civil War had split and devastated the brothers. Breed was the sole survivor. His mother, a God-fearin' woman, had died within a fortnight after President Lincoln's address. Breed was tough and had the grit and savvy to stay alive.

As Breed trotted through the fort's gate he saw a knot

of men gathered by the feed shed. Sergeant Fitz was the center of attention with Corporal Calhoun as supporting cast. Breed led his mount toward Fitz.

"Thanks for the help back there, Sergeant." Sarcasm laced Breed's voice.

"No problem, Breed," retorted Fitz. "We saved the wagons. That's what is important. Besides, we knew you could handle all them Injuns."

Corporal Calhoun chimed in. "Anytime we can help again, let us know." He hammed it up much to the delight of the followers.

Breed tipped his hat, turned away, and rode to the stables. As he dismounted Stills approached him.

"How's all them sergeant's boys doin'?" Stills asked with interest as he watched the group.

"Fine, Dave. They're in rare form. Something on your mind?"

"Which wagon was Fitz driving?"

"I believe it was the rear one. Why?"

"Look at this." Breed followed Dave to the wagons. "This here front wagon is shot full of holes and arrows." After counting eleven bullet holes and six arrows in the lead wagon, Dave looked at Breed. "Fitz's wagon, not a scratch. No holes."

"What do you think, Dave?"

"I cain't put a finger on it, Breed. But somethin' ain't right." Dave was concerned. Breed took note of it.

"I agree, my friend. Let me dwell on it. How many Indians were in your gully? I could swear from all the flying lead there were more than ten as No-Feet said."

12

Dave paused and reflected back on the firefight. He started to answer then hesitated. "By damn, Breed. I was drawin' down on one of those Indians when he shot at me. He never stopped to reload. Some of them boys had repeatin' rifles." Stills pondered the consequences of his statement. "I'd swear on it. I was too busy duckin' bullets but it comes clear now." Dave ran his fingers through his long, unkempt hair.

"That's what I figured. Do you think those Indians on the road could have overtaken the last wagon?"

"Yep, I do. Easily. Guess we are thinkin' the same thing, huh?"

Breed nodded grimly. Those Indians were too well armed. They had a source for rifles. Whether they were trading for them or stealing them, Breed meant to find out.

"Begging your pardon, Sergeant Stalwart. Colonel Prentice would like to see you in his office as soon as possible." The messenger interrupted Breed as he cleaned and oiled his .45–70. Breed set the gun and oil aside and walked with the messenger. They crossed the vast, deserted parade ground and stepped in unison onto the porch of officer country. The soldier knocked sharply on the colonel's door, hesitated a moment, and opened it to announce Breed's arrival. Breed's eyes gradually adjusted to the dimly lighted room.

Colonel Wilbur Neville Prentice II struggled out of the stuffed chair and shuffled from behind his desk. He offered Breed a clammy, limp handshake and motioned him to take a seat. Breed pulled a chair over with his toe, slacked into it, and regarded his commanding officer with barely disguised contempt. The man was on the poor side of forty-five with graying close-cropped hair and white sidewalls. His heavy facial features had settled; puffy, deep-set eyes and fleshy, chipmunk jowls. A combination of poor posture and a paunch made him appear much shorter than his full six-foot height. The man was, in a word, tired.

"Sergeant Stalwart, thank you for coming so promptly." As if I had a choice, Breed jokingly thought. "I heard about the close call with the wagons. I am pleased they weren't damaged or lost. It would be most difficult to replace them. Oh, glad the men got back, too." Breed thought, That's most considerate of you, Colonel.

"Yes, sir," Breed answered automatically. The officers liked that. Made them feel important.

The colonel shuffled to the wall covered with campaign maps. He grabbed a pointer, then searched for several long seconds before pinpointing the location. "You'll select three men besides yourself to provide escort for a wagon coming from Fort Claybourn. Rendezvous tomorrow at approximately thirteen hundred hours here—" He tapped the site on one of the maps. "At Hooks Junction. Return to Fort Manning as expeditiously as possible. I cannot impress upon you too strongly how important it is that this shipment gets through. And I do not want any loose talk either. Understood?"

14

That word grated on Breed. He felt like a child being lectured to. "Yes, sir. May I ask what the shipment is, sir?"

"No," blustered the colonel as he returned to his desk and sat. "You haven't a need to know. Just make damned sure it gets here. I'll leave the petty details to you. That's all. Dismissed."

"Yes, sir." Breed turned toward the door, puzzled and frustrated the colonel didn't confide in him. As he opened the door the colonel reminded him, "Make sure your detail is well chosen and can keep their mouths shut. Understood?"

"Yes, sir." He saluted as he left the room.

Breed knew the colonel had been drinking again. It was barracks knowledge the old man hit the sauce. The colonel's only positive attribute was his decisive demeanor. He made quick decisions, right or wrong, and stuck with them. To try and change his mind was an exercise in futility. Most of the officers felt his uncompromising orders were a result of temper or moodiness brought on by whiskey. Breed felt the man was incompetent and the Army had stationed him at Fort Manning to avoid further embarrassment. By that move the Army had narrowed the odds that Colonel Prentice would make any future military miscalculations.

With No-Feet in the lead, Breed, Stills, and Williams left Fort Manning an hour before sunup. The black sky was faintly cracked with a solitary slate-gray streak.

Crickets sang, as did the occasional mourning dove. The men shivered against the predawn chill. It would be a hard push to Hooks Junction. After a brief rest there, they would rendezvous with the wagon from Fort Claybourn. Each man was lost in his own thoughts. Breed had chosen his veteran soldiers again. Neither Stills nor Williams had asked Breed what it was they were to guard. They knew if Breed had wanted them privy, he would have told them.

Hooks Junction consisted of three wagon ruts that converged in the middle of thousands of miles of barren, wind-blown desert. The patrol came within sight of the junction at midday. Breed and Stills swept the left fork and skirted Buffalo Hump. No-Feet and Williams covered the right fork. They met on the Fort Claybourn rut.

"Nothin', boss," Williams reported. "I never saw a livin' critter out there." Will talked around the toothpick.

"I had to make sure," Breed answered with a smile. "Colonel Prentice must have his brass birds at stake over this one. He's taking no chances. I cannot tell you what we are escorting. I don't know either. I will tell you one thing certain," he warned them. "Our butts are on the line." The soldiers rode off the road a short distance and ate lunch by a small spring. Breed wearily dismounted and stretched his legs. "Let's have some coffee while we wait."

After a sparse lunch the men relaxed with cups of coffee. No-Feet was an Apache who truly enjoyed coffee. He put two heaping spoonfuls of sugar in every cup. The scout sat apart from the soldiers: he was aloof but listened carefully to any conversation made. No-Feet trusted no one and relied entirely upon himself. When he had something to say he spoke, otherwise he remained silent. Breed knew that although No-Feet disliked and distrusted the soldiers, his burning hatred for other Indians made him collaborate with the white man.

Several years past No-Feet had refused to ride with renegade young bucks on a wagon-train raid. Broken Arm, brother of Walking Tall, had called him a coward and a squaw woman, and had talked with contempt about him in front of his people. Then, when No-Feet was out with a war party, Broken Arm had shamed the brave's squaw and cast her out of camp. She'd died trying to reach No-Feet. Weeks later Walking Tall's braves had found what was left of Broken Arm. His body was so brutally mutilated the Indians spoke with admiration about the deed. There was not a track to be found. No clues as to the identity of the murderer of Broken Arm. Hence the name, the man who walks with no feet. Breed had two strong feelings about this Apache. He was relieved to have him on the Army's side and he hoped never to have No-Feet tracking him.

A feather-thin dust plume betrayed the wagon's approach.

"Saddle up, men," Breed told his troopers. "We'll fill our canteens at Hooks Spring. Better water there."

By the time the men leisurely watered their mounts

and filled canteens, the point rider came into view. The man cautiously worked his way through the arroyos and methodically checked the terrain. He stayed on the high ground while being careful not to silhouette himself against the skyline. Breed watched him intently and noted his style. A. D. Fuller. One of the Army's topnotch scouts. Breed smiled and thought, Must be important cargo to send the very best.

The detail met the wagon. A.D. and Breed exchanged barbs. A.D. introduced him to Lieutenant Dirk Flapton. The young officer was an experienced, confident Indian fighter. His eyes revealed much. He was constantly searching, on guard, and alert to his surroundings. Breed saluted the officer and received a snappy salute in return.

"James Stalwart," the officer commented. "I've heard tall tales from A.D. concerning you. I'm pleased to meet you."

"Don't believe A.D., sir. You will be better off," Breed added, a dig at the other scout.

"Good. Now, Sergeant, fill me in on the second half of our trip."

Breed was relieved Lieutenant Flapton was a man of action. With A.D. and No-Feet scouting, Breed's detail would provide roving security to cover more ground. The officer's no-nonsense attitude was refreshing. Within minutes the reinforced detail was on its way toward Fort Manning.

Buffalo Hump. The prominent landmark that overshadowed Hooks Junction. No-Feet waited as Breed rode onto the upper shelf of the dome-shaped butte. When Breed reined in, No-Feet slid off his pony, and knelt by a fresh set of foot and hoof prints.

"How long ago?" Breed asked the Apache.

"Maybe twenty minutes."

A creeping fear nipped at Breed. Whoever had ridden the horse watched the progress of the wagon and detail. Either Breed or No-Feet should backtrack the prints. They had but four hours of daylight. Breed mentally searched their route for an ambush site and thought Cathedral Pass with its surrounding bluffs the likely spot. It would be close to dark when the detail arrived there. Counting on the Indian superstition of not fighting at night, Breed knew if they could last until dark the imminent danger would pass.

Breed mounted and headed for the rutted road. No-Feet followed. As they rode off Buffalo Hump they saw a boiling cloud of dust in the distance. The last thing they'd expected was to be attacked from the rear. Precious little time separated the riders from the wagon. Both horses responded to their urgings and charged from the sloping margin of the hump. On the road, they galloped hard after the detail. Minutes later Breed shouted to the lieutenant.

"Where and how many, Breed?" The lieutenant already anticipated trouble.

"We don't have time to set a defensive perimeter, sir." He pointed to the dust of the approaching riders. "I have an idea. It's all or nothing."

The lieutenant listened as Breed outlined his plan.

"Sounds good to me. Let's do it." The officer was in motion as he snapped orders to his men.

The wagon was pulled into a gully and butted against the bank. The four-horse team was unhitched, picketed, and guarded further back in the gully. Their backs protected by the embankment, and with a clear field of fire, the lieutenant and his six men prepared to defend the wagon. Breed and No-Feet tied their horses with the team and ran several hundred yards to the left of the wagon. They stationed themselves on the steep hillside of the gully they shared with the wagon. Stills and Williams went an equal distance to the right in the same gully and dug in beneath a rock outcropping. If Breed's plan worked, these four soldiers would stop all encircling movements and pinch in the flanks. If it failed, the soldiers and wagon would be surrounded. There would be no survivors. A.D. was out front and would miss the action.

Breed removed three rounds from his cartridge belt and stuck them between the fingers of his left hand. Best make these count, he thought. No-Feet was similarly prepared. They concentrated on the gully.

An eerie quiet settled the air as the soldiers waited. Doubts and incertitude crept into Breed's head. Second choices and alternative plans cast a pall over his decision. He sat motionless. A bead of sweat trickled down his forehead, ran along his nose, and dropped onto his chest. It was too late to change plans. Breed crouched behind a clump of dried grass and glanced toward the distant road. The size of the raiding party stunned him.

He counted twenty riders on the road and four covering each flank. Several Mexicans rode in the main body. Breed watched as four flankers headed his direction. He slipped deeper into the hillside cover. The sound of galloping horses drew nearer and both men cocked their hammers. Four riderless horses thundered around the horseshoe-shaped corner of the sandy gully.

"Oh shit! We've been suckered," he shouted to No-Feet, and stood. As he moved, the torso of an Indian slipped from under the neck of the last pony. The brave smoothly drew an arrow back in his stubby bow. Violently Breed hurled himself sideways to the ground. *Thud!* The arrow nicked his pant leg and buried itself feather deep into the hillside. Breed scrambled to his knees and shot at the thick of the pony's neck. The poor critter went down hard. The Indian rolled onto the sand, leapt to his feet, and sprinted for a side gully. No-Feet's rifle deafened Breed. The brave pitched forward and slammed headfirst into the rocky wall. Slowly he slid onto the sand. His right foot twitched in a dying man's St. Vitus's dance.

Breed crawled to where he had fallen and quickly sifted through the sand for shells. He found one, flipped open the trapdoor, and reloaded. A sixth sense made him look over his shoulder at the ridge. He saw the forehead of an Indian outlined against the sky. With the sight bead below the ridgeline, Breed squeezed off the round. The heavy slug exploded through the dirt, taking everything behind with it.

Breed beckoned to No-Feet. They cut diagonally

across the hillside. After covering thirty yards Breed indicated to the Apache to be ready for a quick charge over the ridge. Breed mouthed, *One, two, three.* They hurdled the sandy ridge. The other side was deserted. Traces of blood speckled the ground. Footprints in the sand led back to the horseshoe corner around which the ponies had charged. Side by side Breed and No-Feet bounded off the soft slope to the gully bottom. Breed cautiously peered around the corner. He was astonished. The dead Indian was gone. The only trace was a dark splotch of blood in the sand, flies swarming on it. The men crossed the gully. Footprints led into a steep, rocky gash and vanished into one of the many directionless arroyos.

"I don't understand, No-Feet. I have never seen Indians so concerned with recovering their dead."

"They hide something."

Intense fire from the wagon brought Breed and No-Feet into action. It sounded like the battle for the wagon was well under way. They double-timed along the gully and found a small game trail that ultimately gave them the advantage of high ground. The two winded soldiers reached the protection of a large boulder and watched as the Indians withdrew from the wagon fight. The Indians took their dead and wounded. They unwillingly left three dead behind. The soldiers in the back of the wagon fired in well-disciplined volleys. Lieutenant Flapton had realized the seriousness of the situation and ordered the crates opened. The precious cargo had been Winchester repeating rifles. The

Indians could not challenge the resulting firepower, and that, combined with the failure of their flanking attack, caused them to retreat.

The silence was almost painful. Breed could hear his heart thump while he gulped in mouthfuls of fresh air. The smell of gunpowder was overwhelming. The two waited until the air cleared before they approached the wagon. Lieutenant Flapton was propped against the far side of the wagon, his shoulder bloodied from a bullet wound, his arm in a sling. A look of stubborn determination on the lieutenant's face told Breed he would never relinquish command of his cargo or men.

The lieutenant glanced at Breed and smiled. He spoke. "The well-kept secret is out. Winchesters. What do you think of them?" His voice contained a trace of excitement.

Breed grabbed one of the rifles. He hefted it, measured length, weight, then shouldered it. "Nice," he answered. "Too light for me, but damn don't they shoot. You knew your cargo?" he questioned the officer. "Bet you never thought you'd use them."

"Right. I wonder how Colonel Prentice will requisition more ammunition."

Breed glanced into the bed of the wagon. It was covered with empty shells.

"Let's have a muster to see how we fared." The lieutenant's suggestion brought the desired results. The soldiers carried out their duties without any prodding from the officer.

No-Feet searched the dead Indians. Breed joined

him. The Apache toed one of the bodies onto his back and carefully studied him. "Not from here. Down south," he told Breed.

"Why do you say that?"

"Mexican Indian. Mud color, stepped-on face, squatty body. Different clothes. Pants are doubled," he added.

"Lots of Indians wear leather pants," Breed answered him.

"These are doubled," No-Feet explained as he squatted and tugged on the pant leg. "The cactus is much higher and will reach the leg of a mounted brave. The doubled leather protects them. He comes from Guerrero or Chihuahua."

"What in the hell they doin' this far north? What do they want?" Breed looked at No-Feet for an answer.

"Rifles," retorted the Indian.

"Damn, they must want them badly to come this far. Suppose someone's selling rifles to them?"

The Apache shrugged his shoulders. It was no concern of his where the Indians were getting their rifles. He would kill them anyway.

"That one"—No-Feet pointed to a body partially hidden behind a large yucca—"is a Comanchero. From Mexico also."

Two shots echoed off in the distance. "That's A.D. Hope he's all right," Breed spoke.

"He will return," No-Feet flatly stated.

Movement to the right startled Breed. He turned sharply and brought his rifle up. *"Con calma,"*

Williams chided him through clinched teeth, a rough-cut toothpick stuck in the corner of his mouth. He had a bandanna bound tightly around his thigh to stop blood seeping from an arrow wound. A strip of shirt was wrapped about Stills's forehead. His sun-bleached hair was matted with blood, and dried blood was caught in his bushy handlebar mustache. Dave's right hand was bloodied and bound. Breed hustled to Williams's side. Together with Stills they walked him to the wagon. "Damn, lads. Why didn't you call for help?"

"We held our own," Stills retorted briefly.

Breed laughed, not able to keep a straight face. "You could have fooled me. Maybe it's best you didn't call." Stills cracked a smile.

The wagon looked like a field hospital. Five of Lieutenant Flapton's troopers were hurt. Three had gunshot wounds, the other two hit by arrows. The men with gunshots were quickly tended to, their wounds cleansed, dressed, and bandaged. Thankfully none of the troopers was seriously injured. The arrow wounds required careful attention. The feathered end of the arrow needed to be broken off before the shaft could be pulled through the wound. Breed faced the two resigned soldiers.

"Boys, I hate to do this. You realize it has to be done. Does anyone have some whiskey?" No one answered. "Speak up, lads. It could save this man's life. Don't worry about regulations," Breed snapped angrily. "Who has some?"

Mace, one of the wounded troopers, pointed his chin toward his horse and saddlebag.

The arrow protruded completely through Mace's thigh. Breed knew the pain must be terrible. It would not be difficult to remove the arrow. Breed positioned the trooper on a rifle box in front of the wagon wheel. He spread Mace's arms and lashed them to the wheel rim. Breed offered him a drink of whiskey. The soldier took a long pull. No-Feet placed a piece of rifle sling in Mace's mouth for him to bite on. Breed firmly held the shaft with both hands. A quick snap and he broke off the feathers. The trooper strained against the leather straps.

"Good lad. It won't take much longer," Breed comforted him. "You all right?" Mace nodded, sweat dripping off his forehead. Breed smoothed the splintered end, then grasped the bloody arrowhead. "Ready?" Mace nodded again. Breed slapped him sharply across the face. The soldier was so startled at being slapped he didn't realize the arrow was out until Breed held it in front of him. "Hold on a bit longer," Breed cautioned him, and poured the whiskey into the seeping wound.

Mace went rigid, writhing in agony as the whiskey flushed the wound. After a full minute he relaxed, tears streaking his face. Breed removed the leather from the trooper's mouth and offered him the bottle. No-Feet cut his wrists free. Mace slumped against the wheel drained of all energy. Breed took two long strips of torn shirt and quickly bandaged the wound.

Mace briefly raised his head and looked Breed in the

eye. "Thanks, Sarge. I think the cure is worse than getting shot."

Breed patted him on the shoulder and turned to face Hawkins, the last wounded trooper. Hawkins squirmed and stood up. "Stay the hell away from me," he shouted. "Keep your hands off me."

Breed was a step ahead of Hawkins and anticipated his move. Breed hit the soldier squarely on the chin with a whistling right hand. Hawkins was out before he kissed the sweet earth. Breed carefully opened the trooper's shirt. The arrow had entered underneath his collarbone. The arrowhead was detectable beneath Hawkins's shoulder blade as a small lump. Breed used his knife and cut delicately into the bulge. When the blade hit the arrowhead, he stopped.

"Stretch him across these two boxes with the arrow over the crack," Breed instructed his helpers.

Positioning the trooper as directed, two soldiers firmly held his arms. Breed straddled Hawkins, placed both hands on the shaft, and pushed firmly. The arrow went in an inch deeper. "Roll him on his side," Royal instructed. Breed could see the arrowhead. It protruded from Hawkins's back. He snapped the feathers off and pulled the shaft through. "Hold him right there, lads." Breed used the whiskey to rinse both entry and exit wounds. "We'll patch him where he lays."

When Hawkins was bandaged Breed leaned against the wheel totally exhausted. He took a long drink from the bottle. The whiskey burned on the way down. Like a glowing ember it settled in his stomach. A mellow feeling replaced the fire and he relaxed. Breed sloshed whiskey on his bloody hands and scrubbed with determination until they came clean. He wiped them dry on his pants. A.D. rode quietly into the camp and silently slipped out of his saddle. He sidled next to Breed. "You need help? Appears to be under control."

"Thanks anyway, A.D. We're finished and ready to ride."

"You needn't burden yourself with worry over those three Indians," A.D. commented with a smile. "I dinged two. The wounded one hightailed it."

"Good work. Mount up the men, A.D. You ready, Lieutenant?"

The lieutenant fought off sweeping waves of pain and gamely replied, "We're ready when you are."

The wounded men rode in the back of the wagon and rested as comfortably as possible. Breed had mustered the remaining soldiers and designated responsibilities for the trip to Fort Manning. A.D. and No-Feet rode point. Stills and Williams, although wounded, covered the flanks. They refused to ride in the wagon. Breed was rearguard along with two of Lieutenant Flapton's troopers.

The soft touches of sunset bathed the harsh yellow desert in gentle red and gold hues. Within minutes it was dark. With a wool-lined jacket to cut the chill, Breed rode wearily into the starry night. He was too tired to be hungry and too beat to care. The detail moved along well as the horses sensed they were close to home. Breed trotted past the wagon. The driver was asleep, slack reins in hand. The wounded soldiers were in various stages of painful sleep. All anxiously awaited the end of the torturous ride. Breed urged his horse forward and caught No-Feet. The Apache looked like a blanket-wrapped squaw.

"Who do you think watched us from Buffalo Hump this morning?"

"No Indian. Too sloppy and no Indian pony. It was a big man. The tracks were deep in the sand."

"If it wasn't an Indian, who in the hell was it?" Breed sought an answer.

"Don't know."

The detail struggled into Fort Manning before midnight and headed directly for the infirmary. Breed was relieved to see Doctor "Sawbones," R. W. Fullbright. Although the doc complained about the hour and the number of wounded, he had them inside and mothered shortly after their arrival. Breed delivered the rifles to the armory and put them under lock and key. He secured quarters for the lieutenant's soldiers and dropped the wagon and team off at the stable. Dead on his feet, Breed stumbled to his quarters and fell onto his cot completely beat.

CHAPTER
2

Ten minutes after Breed's detail left that morning for Hooks Junction and the rendezvous, a solitary figure slipped away from Fort Manning. Three loose logs behind the armory served as the secret exit. They were now back in place, invisible except to someone intentionally searching for them. The beefy man hurried toward the stand of pine at the far end of the plateau. There a hobbled horse waited. From the fort, a sentry covering that quadrant prayed for the safe departure of the shadowy figure. A fairly substantial monetary return depended upon no alarm being sounded.

The lone rider followed the detail. He forced himself not to become overanxious and blunder onto the detail's rearguard. At each natural swell in the road the rider cautiously approached the crest, removed his hat, and slowly topped the rise. His eyes were fixed ahead as he searched for the soldiers. If he was seen, heads would roll, and his would be the first. By midday the detail had reached Hooks Junction. The rider turned away shy of the crossroads and headed for the backside of Buffalo Hump. He zigzagged onto the Hump, nudged his horse onto a small bench, and dismounted. A spindly, gnarled cedar gave him good cover. The man settled down and waited for the soldiers to make the next move.

After midday the man watched as the detail mounted

and rode for the rendezvous with the wagon. A smile cracked his mouth. Everything was going according to plan. He left his cover and ducked around the corner to face Mexican Hat Rock. He removed a small mirror from his pocket and flashed several long signals toward the rock. No movement. Had he missed them? Bellying down he methodically searched every rock and piñon with the glasses. No one.

"Damn it, Campesino! Where in the hell are you?" he muttered in frustration.

It had been prearranged that Campesino and his men would wait on Mexican Hat Rock for the mirror signal. From there they would catch and ambush the wagon. Their reward would be thirty new Winchester repeating rifles and ammunition. This plan had taken two months to materialize due to a delay in the shipment of the rifles. Campesino should have quietly waited across the border. Instead of lying low, he'd raided and killed at random along the border.

"Ah hell," the rider complained. "I'm dead. Thirty ounces of his gold and no damned wagon to show for it."

He returned to his tethered horse with anger of defeat and mounting frustration. The wagon and detail were moving again. He watched in dismay as the Indian scout turned and rode in his direction. The man was forced to abandon his location. He followed his tracks off Buffalo Hump and headed for the deep arroyos that fanned out from the higher ground. To hell with covering his tracks, there was no time. He doubted he would be followed, as the detail was short-handed. After reaching the bottom of the arroyo he rode into a steep-walled canyon and dismounted. The man climbed the rocky wall, doubled back, and settled beside a boulder that overlooked his original trail. From here he could make sure he wasn't being followed. When the Apache and scout looked in his direction, he pressed into the hillside, and silently prayed they would not follow. Much to his relief they mounted and rode off the Hump.

Minutes later the man returned to Buffalo Hump and searched desperately for Campesino and his men.

"Hot damn," he exclaimed with muffled voice. "There they are."

A cloud of dust rose from Mexican Hat Rock. He confirmed with his glasses the riders were Campesino and his men. He snatched the mirror from his pocket and flashed at the riders. After another look he guessed it would take the riders at most a half hour to reach him. Time was running out. The wagon and detail had a good lead. It was essential to intercept them before dark. The man sacrificed caution for speed as he rode off of the hump toward the road.

Campesino and his men slacked off from a hard gallop into a trot. They surrounded the rider, their horses lathered and winded. A damned motley-lookin' bunch, the rider thought. The majority of the men were Mexican Indians, of short stature with mahogany-hued skin. Coarse, long black hair outlined their broad faces. Six Comancheros escorted Campesino through the circle of Indians to further box in the rider. The "pure bloods" contrasted sharply with the Indian "peasants." The Comancheros were lighter skinned with closely chiseled features. Their size alone set them apart from the Indians. To a man the Comancheros rode the finest horses—no doubt stolen. Each man's saddle was hand-crafted and ornately decorated. Bandoleros of shells were draped over their shoulders. This raiding party was heavily armed and spoilin' for a fight.

A scruffy white man rode next to Campesino.

"Hello, Lacy," the rider spoke. "Fine-lookin' crew you got here."

"Hey, turncoat," Lacy hissed back, "any one of these boys would just as soon slit your throat as look at you. So cut the shit."

"You're late. Guess that's to be expected from a bunch of outlaws. And not a one smart enough to—"

The last words hadn't left the man's mouth before a sledgehammer blow knocked him out of his saddle to the ground. Rising to his knees he cupped his throbbing ear and searched for the source of the blow. One of the Comancheros smiled down at him. In the Mexican's right hand was a short whip. A trainman's watch slowly spun as it dangled from the other hand.

"Oye, Señor Lacy." The Comanchero with the whip spoke. "I donna theenk thees estupid eshit nosa how time eet ees." Lacy laughed wickedly.

The downed rider fully realized how far he had overstepped himself. He removed his bloodied hand and collected his courage. "I know what you're thinkin', Lacy.

Remember, if you kill me, you won't get any more rifles," the rider pleaded his case, his life hanging in the balance. "Don't cut off the source that supplies you."

Lacy gave him a chilling stare and turned to Campesino. Lacy spoke in Spanish to the solid block of a man who sat impassively, his face expressionless. Campesino's thick features were shaded by heavy brows. A flat nose and slash mouth added credence to an already ruthless reputation. His ebony eyes burned at the rider while Lacy spoke.

Campesino listened fully before he spoke. *"Buena, muchachos. Buscamos los soldatos,"* he addressed the Comancheros. His soft voice and gentle manner were out of character. The Comancheros gave their leader unanimous nods of approval. Campesino then spoke to his compadres in Apache. Grunts of approval were their answer.

"How far gone is the wagon? A quarter hour?" Lacy questioned.

"More like half. They wasn't wastin' no time. You'll have to ride like hell to catch them."

"Well, thank you, traitor," Lacy berated him. "We intend to do just that. Nice doin' business with you."

"Vamos," was the single command from Campesino as he nudged his pony forward. The Indians scattered on the road. The Comancheros followed close behind.

The Comanchero with the whip had not moved, and smiled sympathetically. "Es timee to go. *Adios, amigo.*"

As he yanked his horse around, he slashed viciously

at the standing figure. The whip smacked the man on his right buttock cheek, ripped his pants, and drew blood. The now-solitary figure daubed at the fresh wound and plodded slowly to his waiting horse. His shirt, sweat-soaked and sour-smelling, stuck to his back. He had come within a trigger pull of dying there with the wind-blown tumble weeds. The ride back to Fort Manning would be a long one.

The morning following the ambush and fight, the messenger tried to shake Breed awake. Normally at the slightest touch or noise Breed woke, but he was exhausted from the day before. The messenger persisted. "Sergeant Stalwart. Colonel Prentice requests you join him in his office immediately."

"What time is it?" he managed to ask.

"Six o'clock, Sergeant. I might add that the C.O. is in a nasty mood."

"Thanks, private. Appreciate the warning. I'll be there shortly."

Breed did not bother to dress; he had slept in his clothes. What could be of such vital importance this early in the day? "Who knows," he talked to himself. "For that matter, who cares? I've given up trying to second-guess that man." Minutes later Breed knocked on the office door and was growled in. Once inside he glanced around the room and saw Lieutenant Flapton, Sergeant Fitz, and several captains from Cavalry and Artillery present. He saluted the colonel and received a fierce return salute.

"Sit down, gentlemen." Colonel Prentice paused. "I'm wrought up concerning this dereliction of duty. I have half a dozen wounded troopers in the infirmary and one to bury. There is a wagonload of rifles that were not to be opened, let alone fired"—he cast a withering glance at Lieutenant Flapton—"and not a single report on my desk. Can anyone tell me why?" He demanded an answer.

No one spoke. A stressed silence fell over the room. The commanding officer paced in front of the assembled soldiers, then plopped angrily into his chair. Lieutenant Flapton sat in pain. His head bobbed and dropped, then jerked upright again. The officer's face was drawn, deep circles shadowing his bloodshot eyes. Breed made a move to spare him further pain. "Sir, I will accept full responsibility—"

The office door exploded open, banging loudly against the wall. In stormed Doc Fullbright. He was outraged, his fury spilled over. He strode to the colonel's desk, placed both hands upon it, and met Prentice eyeball to eyeball. In barely controlled rage he spoke, "If you ever move a wounded man out of my infirmary again without my express consent, I'll personally wrap your ass in a sling and shit-can it. Is that clear enough to understand, Colonel Prentice?"

Prentice was a fool, but he knew better than to countermand Sawbones. He merely nodded consent. The doctor walked to Lieutenant Flapton and helped him to his feet. Together they exited the stilled room.

Colonel Prentice, embarrassed in front of the men,

tried with partial success to regain the lost initiative. "As you were saying, Sergeant Stalwart."

"Sir, I dropped off Lieutenant Flapton and the other wounded at the infirmary well after midnight. After depositing the rifles in the armory and securing quarters for the men, I turned in. I didn't feel it was imperative at—"

"I'll decide what's important at this fort, Sergeant," the colonel interrupted him.

"Yes, sir. I'll get right on the report."

"You're damned right you will," Prentice thundered. "I will not tolerate slipshod military behavior at my fort. Not while I am in command. Understood?"

Sergeant Fitz asked a question to break the chill. "This oversight won't go in services records, will it, sir? It would be a real—" Sergeant Fitz was cut off.

"I've already taken the matter under consideration. Thank you, Sergeant Fitzpatrick, for your interest. Gentlemen." The colonel nodded curtly. "Dismissed."

Once outside, Breed confronted Sergeant Fitz. "Keep your concerns to yourself next time, Fitz. I don't need your kind of help."

"Don't you tell me what to do, Stalwart," the big Irishman blustered.

That night two soldiers smuggled the thirty new rifles out of the fort's armory. The bolts that secured the rear window in place had been sawn through. The steel window frame was easily removed. Entry into the rifle boxes had been a cinch. When Lieutenant Flapton used the rifles at the ambush site, the government seals had been broken. Colonel Prentice had ordered new wire seals placed on the boxes, but the thieves cut the wires close to the latches to gain access. Once the rifles were removed, the wires were put back in place. A mixture of grease and charcoal was rubbed into the cuts, hiding them from all but the closest inspection.

The two men positioned the rear window in place before moving to the gap in the fort's log wall. They handed the last four rifles through to the cowboy who waited outside. "That's all," whispered the bigger of the soldiers. "We're even, Lacy. Thirty rifles for thirty pieces of gold. A hell of a deal if I say so myself."

"Right. Pleasure doin' business with you blue-boys. I wouldn't go pokin' my nose 'round these parts for a spell. Blue is the wrong color to be."

The cowboy slipped into the darkness while the men replaced the logs in the wall. The big man weighed the cowboy's words carefully. "Lad, that sounds like good advice. I believe the man." The other man grunted in agreement.

Colonel Prentice stacked the last of his messages and papers on the desk. One of those messages was a direct order from General W. W. Harvey at Fort Wallace. He wanted more cavalry action, escorts for wagon trains, and guard details. The general wanted high visibility to reassure the settlers, cattlemen, and wagon trains that the U.S. Army was in control of the vast region. The southwest district, which included Fort Manning, was to bare the brunt of these new actions. The orders also implied the soldiers were to attack any "targets of opportunity."

Prentice leaned back in his worn leather chair, propped his feet on the desk, and pondered these "targets of opportunity." With the new rifles a quick strike at the Indians might readily serve his career. A lightning raid would look good on his record, and could conceivably expedite a transfer out of this dusty hellhole. Intrigued by the idea, he left his chair and walked to the map-covered wall. Visions of past U.S. Army successes swept through his mind. Horseshoe Creek, Table Mesa, Chihuajota. All were decorated battles between the Army and the savages. The names of the commanding officers who'd led these campaigns were burned in Colonel Prentice's memory: Major Reynolds, Captain Wells, and Lieutenant Enright. A smoldering jealousy gnawed at Prentice's innards. One more name could be on that list. His. He would issue orders from here and wait as they were carried out to a successful conclusion. It would have to be a quick raid. Hit the hostiles before they knew what happened. Get out before they could recover.

"Campaign Twin Buttes. Commanding Officer, Colonel Neville Prentice," the colonel gloated as he pinpointed the landmark on the map. "Sounds like an excellent location to go down in history as another sound U.S. Army victory. With those new Winchester rifles we could handle one hundred Indians," he boasted.

Colonel Prentice had lost touch with reality in his whiskey-soaked delusions of grandeur. Twin Buttes was the very heart of Indian country. The buttes were sacred ground to the Indians. They owned them. This was the land of their forefathers, their ancestral inheritance, and the home of their gods. As far as was known, only one white man had ever reached Twin Buttes and lived to tell about it.

The colonel went to his shelf and pulled a thick, leather-bound volume from the stack of books. At his desk he thumbed through the notes and articles about Twin Buttes. One of the newspaper headlines caught his eye.

GOLD AT TWIN BUTTES!

This was how the *Nuevo Loredo Star* had bannered the expedition's story. The account of fifteen prospectors who had left Ojo Prieto for Twin Buttes. The tales of Spanish gold and treasure were legend. Rumor was, the Seven Cities of Cibola were there. The hooplaed departure of this heavily armed and drunken party had added to the carnival atmosphere. The buttes were a full three days' ride from the wind-ravaged adobe hovel that was Ojo Prieto, a stage relay station.

Two weeks after the prospectors' departure, an overland stage picked up a terribly mutilated and crazed straggler wandering in the desert. The man ranted and raved about Indians and Twin Buttes. Wiley Hobart, the horse doctor at Ojo Prieto, nursed him back to

health. People disregarded the man's delirious gib-
berish as crazy talk and some thought him possessed.
Wiley listened patiently and believed his horror stories
as truth. One night as the survivor related a particular
experience to Wiley, he suddenly jumped to his feet,
screamed at the top of his lungs, and fell stone dead on
the ground.

Perhaps the Indians let the white man go as a living
example so he could spread the word. And from that
day hence, no white man had ever ventured close to
Twin Buttes. It was conceded to the Indians. The sole
survivor of the Twin Buttes expedition had been buried
fifty-eight years ago.

The colonel set the book on his desk and returned to
plot his quest of victory. "All the more reason to take
our battle there," the man rambled on. "Strike them
where they least expect it." Another sip from the glass
further fortified the commanding officer and convinced him that Twin Buttes was a brilliant choice.

Lieutenant Albright removed the double locks from the
heavily reinforced armory door and stepped inside.
Why in the hell Colonel Prentice wanted to reinventory
the Winchester ammunition was beyond reason. It had
been done only last week. As Lieutenant Albright
squeezed between the stacked rifle boxes, his foot
slipped into a crack and threw him off balance. His
resulting fall knocked over three boxes. The officer
struggled to his feet and quickly realized the crates
were empty. He knocked half a dozen over in blind

panic. "My God," he cried out, "they're gone." Those rifles are gone. So is my military career. He was horror-struck at the thought.

The young officer ran to the logbook in hopes of finding a new entry but knowing it wouldn't be there. "I've got to tell Colonel Prentice. Right away," he talked to himself as he headed out of the building.

The lieutenant slammed the door and hurriedly hooked one lock in place. He snatched his hat from his head and sprinted for the commanding officer's office. Fear gripped his shaking legs as he stood before the colonel.

"You are out of uniform, Lieutenant." The colonel reprimanded him for not having his shirt tail tucked in and for not having his hat on. "Now, what did you say about the rifles?"

"Missing, sir," repeated the lieutenant.

"The hell you say," roared Colonel Prentice. "Impossible!"

"Sir, I just came from the armory. The new shipping crates are empty. The seals are broken. There isn't a Winchester there."

"Damn you," cursed Colonel Prentice. "I'll have your butt for this. And your commission! You can count on that." The colonel stabbed a finger at the young officer.

The lieutenant had not moved. He stood ramrod straight and took the tongue-lashing.

"Hellfire, man. Don't just stand there. Get the gunnery officers and Sergeant Stalwart. Meet me at the armory. Pronto!" The colonel was in motion.

"Yes, sir," Lieutenant Albright blurted as he followed the colonel out the door.

Breed and Lieutenant Albright hustled to the armory. Colonel Prentice paced back and forth awaiting the arrival of the lieutenant. It was all he could do to control his rage.

"The key, man. *The key!*" He shouted in anger.

Lieutenant Albright searched through his pockets before he found the key. He managed to open the lock on the third try. The colonel brushed him aside and charged through the door. He went directly to one of the empty crates. "It's empty," he roared.

No shit. I told you the rifles were gone. The lieutenant fought back the impulse to tell him exactly that.

"Gentlemen"—the commanding officer spoke with theatrical gravity—"we have a serious military theft on our hands. If in fact the rifles are missing, it is imperative we discover how they were stolen and recover them as quickly as possible. Split up. Search every board in this building. Lieutenants Albright and Burns, examine all the flooring planks. Sergeant Stalwart, check each and every log in the walls." The colonel pointed as he assigned responsibilities. "Sergeant Fitz, the window and door. Lieutenant Hancock, the ceiling." The colonel was once again the Prentice of old, snapping orders and in full command.

Breed glanced at Fitz. From where had he materialized? Lieutenant Albright had not requested his presence. The men went about inspecting their assigned areas. Breed scoured the entire length of one wall. He pushed, scratched, and searched the logs for any weakness or tampering. The mud chinking was solid. He happened to look up as Sergeant Fitz gave the rear window a quick once-over. Fitz did not touch the metal frame in his rush. Breed continued along the wall and checked the logs beneath the rear window. The outer edge of one log was slightly darker than the others. Trailing a wet fingertip on the log, Breed picked up tiny metal filings. He continued his inspection of the remaining walls.

"Well, men?" the colonel questioned anxiously.

"Nothing here, sir," Lieutenant Albright answered as he and Lieutenant Burns replaced the last ammo crate. "The floor is solid." The two were sweat-soaked from lifting the heavy boxes.

"Sir, the ceiling is sound," Lieutenant Hancock stated, and dropped from a rafter. The officer was filthy, cobwebs caught in his hair.

"Damn it all to hell," swore the colonel. "You, Stalwart. Anything?"

"Negative, sir. The walls are secure."

"The window and door are bolted firm, sir," Fitz told the officer.

Colonel Prentice was clearly exasperated. He showed it. "Lieutenant Albright, I want to see you in my office immediately. That's all, gentlemen. Please keep this under your hats for the time being." The officer strode angrily away. He stopped suddenly and turned to speak. "I want this building secured and guarded twenty-four hours a day. For whatever the hell

44

good it will do. I leave the guard schedule to you, Lieutenant Hancock."

"Yes, sir," replied the startled officer.

Breed wanted to see Lieutenant Albright before he left for the meeting with Colonel Prentice. Breed dallied and was the last to leave. As he walked past the officer he spoke softly. "Take your time locking up. I want to check something."

Once outside, Breed watched Sergeant Fitz hurry across the drill field and cut through the parade grounds. With Fitz out of sight he darted between the armory and the supply building and went directly to the rear window. He grabbed the frame with both hands and jerked it free. Just as he had suspected. Breed replaced the window and on a hunch inspected the log wall. He knelt and saw daylight between the logs. A hard push against the logs. Three moved. He trotted back toward the front of the armory and nearly ran over the lieutenant.

"Sir, I discovered how the rifles were stolen. The rear window frame bolts have been cut through. There is an opening in the log wall. Looks like more than one person worked hard to get those rifles out of the armory and through the wall." Breed took the time to explain the theft to the officer. "Tell the colonel you discovered it but didn't want to say anything in front of the men. He'll buy it."

"Thanks, Breed." The lieutenant was visibily relieved. "Any idea who did it? Or why?"

"I'll tell you later. An inside job, no doubt, with

someone who knew about the rifles. I have a few hunches to go on. Get going and don't let the old man badger you."

The stolen rifles were the topic of discussion at evening meal. The contrasts in feelings were as varied as the men involved. Colonel Prentice was concerned with another blemish on his military record and how it might further tarnish his career. A promotion and a sure ticket out of Fort Manning were in jeopardy. Lieutenant Albright knew his fledgling military life was on the line. The stockade at Fort Leavenworth flashed through his mind. Sergeant Fitz was praying he wouldn't have any patrols in the immediate future. Breed feared the worst. He knew where those rifles had ended up. Either Walking Tall or Campesino were justly contented. They were better armed than the soldiers. The casualty rate would reflect the unevened odds.

Two days later the formal inquiry results were released. No action taken. A lack of hard evidence stalled further investigation. Breed mentioned the rear window to Colonel Prentice. "I'll handle it," was his curt reply. As far as Breed knew no action was taken.

The assembled men sat in astoundment. They understood only too well what they had heard. "I will repeat those orders, gentlemen," Colonel Prentice stated proudly, eyes gleaming. "Lieutenant Hobart, with Sergeants Stalwart and Fitz, will form a patrol to reconnoiter Twin Buttes. Army intelligence reports increased activity in that general area. You will make no contact. Observe the hostiles and report to me. Don't misunderstand me . . ." He smiled confidently. "If it becomes necessary to defend yourselves, do so by all means."

Lieutenant Hobart, a wily Indian fighter, stood and cleared his throat. "Begging the colonel's pardon, sir. Are you aware of the fact no white man has ever lived—"

"I am well aware of that fact, Lieutenant."

"With all due respect, sir. Are you also aware of—"

"Lieutenant Hobart," Colonel Prentice, now highly rankled, spoke. "Are you questioning my authority in this matter?"

"No, sir. What I am questioning is your judgment."

The bombshell dropped. No one spoke for several seconds. With his lower lip quivering in rage, the colonel broke the silence. "Lieutenant Hobart, as of now you are relieved of your duties and are on report."

"Thank you, sir." The lieutenant saluted the colonel and left the hushed room.

Colonel Prentice turned to the map. He tapped Twin Buttes sharply with the pointer. He turned slowly and faced the men. "Gentlemen, what we have here is an opportunity to serve history. No!" He stopped and corrected himself. "To make history. Each man has a key role to carry out in this operation. By participating in this challenging mission you will strike into the quick of this Indian uprising. First, by scouting for information and hard intelligence; and second, by administering a sound thrashing to the hostiles. We can take

U.S. Fifth Army A Company colors and show them to the heathens. Impress upon them we are fighting men and are here to stay."

The commanding officer droned on at length. Breed measured the men surrounding him. Most were somber, reflecting inwardly on the de facto death sentence passed upon them by the colonel. Being professional soldiers they accepted their orders. Sergeant Fitz looked afright, as pale as death. Perchance his worst fears about the rifles were about to come true?

". . . again I repeat. Show the colors! Let those savages know who you are. Thank you and good luck. Lieutenant Albright, you will assume command of the patrol. Leave within the next forty-eight hours. Understood?" The lieutenant nodded numbly. Was this the colonel's way of getting back at him for the missing rifles? "Fine. Dismissed."

Sergeant Fitz was the first to break the tomblike silence. He strode boldly forward to offer his congratulations to the colonel on his insight and daring. Several of the officers followed suit to avoid embarrassing Colonel Prentice. Beaming with the pride that his ego coveted, the commanding officer enjoyed one of his finer moments.

The next morning Lieutenant Albright sought out Breed. Together they worked on the multiple tasks involved in requisitioning mounts, arms, ammo, and rations for the patrol. These jobs would take the better part of the day to complete. After the noon meal Lieutenant Albright returned with the muster and hesitantly handed it to Breed. "That's all the manpower I could shanghai. Fine collection, isn't it?" The officer tried to joke about the list.

"Sir." Breed laughed in disbelief. "Half these men don't know if they are the horse or the rider. I guess we're stuck with them, aren't we?"

Lieutenant Albright groped for words. "We have an Italian immigrant who doubles as a bugler, and a German blacksmith."

"Sir, you open for some suggestions?" The officer nodded. He knew Breed's thinking was sound. "We will travel light. At least we can try and be fairly mobile. Nighttime travel. That way we will beat the heat and just maybe have a chance of getting there."

"Sounds good, Breed. Might not hurt to issue some extra ammo on the off chance we run into those Winchesters."

"You bet, Lieutenant. I was thinking the same thing. I'll go see Sawbones and check the F-U list. We ride at sundown."

Fit and Unfit list. This was the infirmary report on those individuals not medically qualified for upcoming duty. It was a battle of wits and con artistry between the soldiers and the doc. With marching orders issued that very day, the walking wounded might've materialized at the infirmary with creative and nearly fatal illnesses. But the odds of hoodwinking Sawbones were slim to none.

"Hi, Doc. Killed anyone lately?" Breed dug at the old man.

"You should talk," he retorted sharply. "You seem to have a talent for leaving death and destruction wherever you go." Breed enjoyed the old-timer. They ribbed each other continually but held a mutual respect for each other.

"How many casualties do we have this morning as a result of the marching orders?"

"Only one, but I think you might be interested. A certain sergeant with a 'severe hearing problem.'" Sawbones could not show Breed the medical log outright but he left no doubt as to the contents. There was an unspoken understanding between field sergeants and the doc concerning medical reports. If a man was legitimately sick, Doc would be the first to put him on report, and relieve him of his duties. If a man was shuckin' him, Sawbones would put the final nail in the coffin lid.

"What's with Fitz's ear? He fabricated a story he was bitten by a horse."

"He said the same thing to me. Came in several days ago and complained that he was stone deaf. It is a nasty cut, but I'll tell you one thing sure . . ." The healer shook his head. "No horse did that. And he has no hearing loss either. He's up to no good and wants to get out of this patrol in the worst way."

"Thanks, Doc. See you soon." Breed then added with uncertainty, "I hope."

"Bring yourself back in one piece, will you? Or should I say, bring yourself back alive. I'll put the pieces back together."

CHAPTER
3

The fourteen soldiers rode out of Fort Manning into the quickly dwindling reddish-pink evening light. The day's blistering heat was broken. A hint of a breeze caressed them. The patrol was spread out, in no fear of ambush. No point or flankers were needed, although No-Feet was out front. The ride to Twin Buttes would take two nights, the patrol arriving there with the second dawn. Traveling by night the horses would not get beaten down by the relentless heat and sun. With skill and a lot of luck they would hit the springs at Sagebrush and Blue Pine mesas at night. Hopefully the men and horses would be rested for the following day's ride to Twin Buttes.

A waxing gibbous moon bathed the desert in a soft, silvery glow. Contrasts between moonlight and pitch-black shadows were sharp and crisp. The soldiers were bundled against the slight chill. Several were asleep in their saddles, their bodies relaxed with the rolling gait of the horses. The only noises were occasional cinch or saddle creakings. Breed was ahead of the pack trying to stay awake as his horse gently rocked him. Suddenly the horse spooked, bringing him alert with a start. A large buck jack rabbit bounded across the road and disappeared under a black sage. Breed let the lieutenant draw alongside. The officer was wrapped in his blanket.

"You alive in there?" Breed questioned softly.

"Uh," grunted the lieutenant. "I think my butt is molded into the saddle." The officer's voice was muffled by the blanket, which covered everything but his eyes.

"We're in good shape, sir. Barring any disasters, we should be in and out of Sagebrush Mesa two hours before sunup. By the time it's light and hot, we'll be in the hills."

"Good. Wake me when we get there."

Although the lieutenant sounded disinterested, he was not. He learned quickly and steadily gained experience needed to stay alive against the Indians. He respected Breed and trusted his judgment. Lieutenant Albright knew Breed had the experience that he, a relatively fresh field lieutenant, lacked but desperately wanted. Together they rode ahead of the other soldiers.

"Did your hunch about the rifles pay off?" the officer asked.

"I don't know, sir. I mentioned the wagon fiasco. The armory window had been tampered with, yet Sergeant Fitz purposely overlooked it. He was the only one who showed up for F and U reports with Sawbones. There isn't a thing I can pin on him. Nothing solid or conclusive."

"I'll admit," laughed the officer, "that when Colonel Prentice mentioned Sergeant Fitz was coming with us, he seemed reluctant as hell to be included in the patrol."

"Can you blame him, sir? He knows where those rifles are," Breed replied with a smile.

"Let's keep a close eye on the 'good sarge.' Also his sidekick, Corporal Calhoun. Those two are entirely too chummy. Always look like they're planning something."

"I agree, sir. Here is what I have in mind for Sagebrush Mesa and the spring." The men talked as they rode.

The spring nestled at the base of Sagebrush Mesa and was hidden in one of the serpentine arroyos that fanned out from the base. The flat-topped mesa, two parade grounds in length, dominated this sector of desolate desert. The mesa stood eighty feet above the desert floor and was readily accessible from all sides. If the spring was clear, the men and horses could rest from the hard ride. Being able to water the horses, and fill water bags and canteens, was a life-or-death necessity if the patrol was to succeed.

The slate-gray bulk of Sagebrush Mesa loomed in front of Breed and No-Feet. From the arroyo, the mesa looked massive and foreboding. Leading their horses on foot they walked up a dry arroyo and rounded each corner only after a thorough check ahead. Every side gully was inspected before they crossed its mouth. They tied their mounts at the base of the mesa. No-Feet disappeared to the left flank. He would cover that side of the mesa. Breed would take the right side. Reaching into his saddlebag, Breed pulled out an old pair of knee-length leather moccasins. He shucked off his boots and slipped into the comfortable softness of the moccasins. By keeping close to the trees Breed traversed the sidehill of the mesa. He cursed the moon-light when he had to cross open ground. Of the numerous trails he found, several led to the summit. None showed any signs of activity. He stepped from rock to rock when crossing the trails, and left no prints.

Breed inched up between two boulders and peered onto the flat mesa-top. He remained motionless. The top was clear. Breed waited until he saw the shadowy figure of No-Feet complete his search before he rose. He slowly stretched his lanky frame to a standing position. Suddenly he realized the figure was not the Apache. He dropped stealthily to the grass and watched with intrigue. The lone figure paused at the edge, looked back toward him, then disappeared. Soon afterward No-Feet came into view in the same vicinity. Breed got to his feet and questioned him. "Where in the hell did he come from?" Breed whispered.

"Don't know. I was after him. He left nothing."

"We'll know by sunrise if he spotted us. The spring clear?" The Apache nodded it was. "Let's go."

"You want me to get him?" the Apache inquired.

"No. It's too late now."

The patrol had dispersed, and covered the hillside of a natural basin. The horses, picketed against a rocky cliff, were shaded and out of view. The men sought shelter under mesquite trees and moved periodically to stay in shadow and keep ahead of the searing sun. By midafternoon the heat was brutal. The air crackled with heat. Shimmering, dancing heat waves distorted everything. The soldiers sweated heavily even while lying in the shade. Breed had had serious misgivings after the patrol left Sagebrush Mesa in the pre-dawn hours. The man on the mesa worried him. If he was an Indian the search was on, but everything had been quiet so far. Blue Pine Mesa was going to be a long shot. A water refill there was of critical importance.

Breed was dozing when No-Feet knelt beside him. Through heavy, lazy eyes Breed realized the Apache had beckoned him to follow. Pushing himself to his feet with considerable effort, he dogged the Apache onto the lip of the bowl. They sat below the ridgeline and looked back toward Sagebrush Mesa. A faint smoke signal was still visible. Glancing at Blue Pine Mesa, Breed saw answering smoke.

"They can't find us before nightfall, can they?"

"No time," replied the Apache with little emotion. "Besides, they wait for tomorrow. As the sun breaks."

Breed looked beyond Blue Pine Mesa to the mirage images of Twin Buttes. "The way we are going now, we'll never make it there."

No-Feet did not respond to the statement, but his look was enough. Now the pressure started. The Indians knew they were in the area. It was a question of finding the soldiers in the myriad of winding arroyos and gullies. The intentional backtracking and apparent aimless wandering of the soldiers last night might delay the Indians, but a blind man could find and follow fourteen shod horses. The general direction of their movement was a dead giveaway. Breed retraced his steps from the ridge and sat dejectedly next to the lieutenant. "Things have gone all to hell, sir. We're in trouble."

"Why's that, Breed?" The heat had sapped the lieutenant's strength as it had done to all the soldiers.

"We are surrounded. Smoke on Sagebrush and Blue Pine mesas. I think we'll be fine tonight, but we are gonna be in tall grass come dawn. There is a slim—and I do mean mighty slim—chance we can get past Twin Buttes before dawn. I hate to say it, but we are running out of choices."

"How far is Blue Pine Mesa from here?"

"Ten of the roughest, most meandering miles you'll ever ride. The buttes are only a few miles beyond. The way it looks to me, either we get caught at Blue Pine Mesa at dawn or we get caught out there later in the day." Breed looked toward the twin mesas as he spoke.

"I'd prefer later in the day," the lieutenant joked. "No sense waiting here to get caught. Let's saddle up."

Twenty minutes later the patrol was moving. The men were loosely bunched. No one wanted to be the straggler who might get picked off. The steepness of the rocky canyon walls precluded use by the Indians. No-Feet was checking ahead, and occasionally climbed to a vantage point. Breed searched cross washes as he looked for traces of campsites or tracks. Two soft dove coos stopped him cold. He sought out the Apache and found him on a ridge crouched behind scattered boulders. Breed tied his horse next to No-Feet's pony and scrambled up the loose, sandy soil. By the time he knelt beside the Apache he was puffing hard. On the other side of the ridge was the dry riverbed that linked Sagebrush and Blue Pine mesas with Twin Buttes. The smaller tributaries fed into this large wash. Six Comancheros were camped on the far side of the wash.

"Oh, *Madre de Dios*," he whispered in disbelief. "I should have guessed it. Campesino's men."

Breed carefully retreated from the ridge without raising any dust. It dawned on him the man they'd seen last night on Sagebrush Mesa was a Comanchero. He reached the floor of the gully and waited for the lieutenant.

"More problems, Breed?" the lieutenant asked as he stopped his horse and dismounted.

"Yes, sir. I'll explain and we'll do some quick planning."

The two squatted while Breed drew a map in the sand. Lieutenant Albright paid close attention to the plan and added several pertinent suggestions. Minutes later they stood. The lieutenant searched for Sergeant Fitz and found him with his entourage sitting off to the side of the wash. "Sergeant, muster the men here and be quick about it." The lieutenant talked in a hushed tone.

The officer and Breed waited patiently until the men were present. "Gentlemen," the lieutenant addressed the soldiers. "We are running out of time and luck. To be blunt, we're trapped. You probably saw or at least know about the smoke signals from both mesas. The

Indians know we are here. They are looking for us at this moment."

The men listened closely as the callow officer spoke. He presented himself well. "To further complicate matters, six Comancheros have set up camp around the far bend." The officer pointed toward the corner. "According to Sergeant Stalwart they are the same bunch that ambushed the rifle wagon several days ago. I don't have to tell you this"—he smiled easily—"they're probably still pissed off about the beating they took. They will be looking for a return favor."

The lieutenant grabbed a long branch and drew the plan of attack in the sand. "Those six are across the riverbed, right there." He stuck the end in the sand. "Sergeant Fitz, you will be in charge of seven men. Your primary responsibility is the horses." The officer pinpointed their location. "It is imperative that you succeed. If you can't catch them, shoot them down. You other men," the lieutenant addressed the cluster of soldiers, "must give the sergeant suppressive fire cover. If he fails, we fail with him."

The officer noticed that several of the men looked bewildered. "I apologize." He laughed. "Throw some lead. Make 'em keep their heads down. Any questions?"

No one answered. As Fitz chose his seven men, Breed stepped forward and spoke. "You remaining men will ride with me. We'll take a crack at those six Mexicans. Mount up!"

The fourteen soldiers mounted in silence; they

understood the dangers. Sergeant Fitz was fearful the Mexicans were armed with a few of the Winchesters. The soldiers were lined abreast and headed toward the mouth of the wash. On the left flank Sergeant Fitz rode with his chosen seven. They would have a straight run at the horses. Hand signals from the lieutenant directed the men into a slow trot, then into a gallop. By the time the soldiers reached the mouth they had formed a passable picket line, and charged full gallop at the Mexicans. Breed, Lieutenant Albright, and the other five soldiers angled slightly to the right in order to have a clear field of fire at the Comancheros.

The soldiers were halfway across the eighty-yard-wide riverbed when the Comancheros heard them. The six froze where they sat. Clearly the last thing they expected to see was a charging line of soldiers bearing down on them. Three Mexicans took a fleeting glance at the soldiers and bolted headlong into the thick underbrush of the riverbank. As the others drew their pistols, a ragged volley rang out from Breed's side of the patrol. When the smoke cleared and the dust settled, the Mexicans were still standing. Breed realized then, his best riflemen were with Sergeant Fitz. He tried to make up for the oversight. He leaned forward slightly, floated with his horse, and shot. One of the Mexicans went down. As Breed reloaded, the man regained his feet.

Several of Sergeant Fitz's men split and bore down on the Mexicans. The Comancheros quickly joined their compadres in the underbrush. The horses panicked and bolted down the riverbed. Stills and Williams skillfully herded them. Breed watched the horses being driven, and hollered to his men to ride away from there. The lieutenant rode alongside Breed and together they peppered the underbrush with their .45's. The Mexicans bellied down and occasionally returned fire.

Breed rode out of pistol range and watched the soldiers ahead in comic disbelief. Trooper Glade and Private Hinton, the dimwits, hadn't yet mastered their mounts. They were holding onto the saddlehorns with both hands, like "city dudes." Breed could see daylight under each one. The alternating rhythm, buttocks smacking against leather, added a strange beat to the stampede. Trooper Opperman, a better blacksmith than a horseman, fared better. He had one hand on the saddlehorn, the other on the cantle. No Mexican could have hit his wildly bobbing body. Corpsman Perkins, a complete stranger to the saddle, alternated between a quick trot and a slow gallop. Private Bancroft, disgusted with the horse he rode, drew up behind Perkins and whipped the corpsman's horse savagely across the rump with his reins. The horse exploded into a full gallop, the corpsman hanging on for his life. Breed couldn't help but remember what the lieutenant had said about these being the best he could find. The attack on the Mexicans should have used two full volleys of ammo. Breed doubted more than eight shots had been fired. But the elements of fear and surprise had worked to their advantage.

The last of the horses and soldiers disappeared beyond the distant corner. Breed noticed the lieutenant was falling behind while trying to ride lightly. "You all right, sir?"

"I was nicked by one of those fliers. I'll make it. Keep moving."

As the lieutenant spurred his mount forward, Breed saw a growing bloodstain covering the area above the officer's hip. Blood covered his buttock and squished between the saddle. The man was dying, Breed thought. He won't last long. Breed galloped ahead for Corpsman Perkins and finally located him. Breed pulled the young man out of line and together they returned to the officer. "Fix him up as best you can, Perkins. We have to keep moving."

"I'll try my best, Sarge," the corpsman replied nervously. "But what should I do?"

"Do?" Breed couldn't believe his ears. "You're the doctor," he snapped. "You damned well better know what to do."

Within a quarter hour the lieutenant rejoined the soldiers. The officer struggled valiantly to keep pace as the patrol rode hard to distance themselves from the Mexicans. The shooting was sure to draw a crowd. Although Perkins had dressed the wound twice, the lieutenant was lagging behind. The officer slowed, then stopped. Pain cut his youthful face. "Breed," he spoke softly, "I'm not going to make it." The lieutenant slid out of the saddle and gradually sank to his knees. "Breed, listen to me." He confronted the scout. "We both know I'm cutting into your chance to escape. Leave me here and carry on."

Breed didn't comment. Everything the officer said was true.

"I have a single request," the lieutenant stated. "Find a good spot overlooking this wash. I want to give you a little breathing room." He added with a wink, "Just in case."

"Yes, sir. I'll rustle one up. Try and take it easy." Breed swung onto his horse and hustled to catch the patrol. He overtook the soldiers within five minutes and rode alongside Sergeant Fitz. "Sergeant, you will be in charge until I return. Follow No-Feet. He knows where to go."

"What's goin' on here? Tell me," Fitz demanded. "I have as much right to know as anyone."

Breed held back the impulse to ride away without giving the sergeant the satisfaction of a reply. He disliked the loutish, surly excuse of a sergeant. "Lieutenant Albright is dying. He wants to set an ambush for either the Comancheros or Indians. If you want my job, have at it."

The big Irishman bristled at the comment, then faced Breed. "You can go straight to hell, Stalwart. I ain't followin' you or no damned Injun anywhere." Sergeant Fitz's ever-present shadow, Corporal Calhoun, consented in silent agreement. "That Injun's yours. You follow him."

"Fine with me, Fitz." Breed dismissed the man. "No-Feet is heading for Blue Pine Mesa. If you want to get there alive, shag him like a twin brother. If you want to go it alone and die out here as buzzard bait, do us all a favor."

Sergeant Fitzpatrick measured Breed's words and reluctantly accepted the truth. His nature did not allow him to give in without a fight. He was the oldest of four boys and had set the example for his siblings. From early childhood he'd learned that if you didn't take something first, someone else would. In primary school, fighting and brawlings had been his forte. Formal education had ended in the fifth grade when he left school to work as a teamster for the freight line. He'd taken continual ribbing about his "carrot top" red hair until he matured and filled out. Lord pity the poor soul who made a comment about it now. At five feet eight inches he was stumpy, a cider keg wide. Tattoos covered both hamhock-sized biceps. He sported a no-neck look combined with a ruddy complexion. The green eyes made the first impression a striking one. Seldom was an excuse needed, or passed by, to get in a fight. It was a way of life for Fitz and he was good at it. He was the consummate brawler and a saloon keeper's dream bouncer.

Breed wheeled his horse and returned to the lieutenant. No-Feet nudged his pony past Sergeant Fitz and headed for Blue Pine Mesa. The Apache glared at the sergeant with hate-filled eyes and passed a death sentence on him. Sergeant Fitz would die for his insulting words. Williams and Stills trailed the Apache. The others moved forward. Fitz turned on his cronies.

"What in the hell you gawkin' at? Go with the red-skin."

While riding to Lieutenant Albright, Breed remembered a small ledge perched above the wash. It would do nicely for the lieutenant, provided he lasted that long. The officer was waiting, reconciled to the hard fact his destiny was to be played out in this nameless arroyo.

"Found your spot, sir. Just a short ride ahead."

"Sounds good, Breed. I'm really hurtin'." Lieutenant Albright winced painfully as he pulled himself into the saddle.

The two men rode through winding gullies to circle behind and climb to the ledge. The officer attempted to dismount but fell heavily out of the saddle. He righted himself by using the stirrup, and leaned against the horse for support. Breed reached to assist him but the officer was steady on his feet.

"This will be fine, Breed. Thanks for the help." The lieutenant put up a good front. "Take my horse. I won't need her. Leave me a canteen, if you wouldn't mind."

Breed was hesitant to take the horse but did so and secured her with a saddle tie. The lieutenant tried several different positions before he bellied down in a shaded indentation. Breed noticed the officer's lower back was blood-soaked, with slow seepage under the bandage. Resting easily, his face no longer etched in pain, Lieutenant Albright spoke. "Oh, that feels so much better," he sighed. "Get going, Breed. And thanks for everything."

"You bet, Tom. Waylay a couple for me." This was the first time Breed had addressed the officer by his first name. It was spoken with respect and admiration. The lieutenant accepted it as offered. Their parting handshake was sincere.

CHAPTER
4

Sergeant Stalwart left the dying Lieutenant Albright to fend for himself. Breed felt a deep loss. The lieutenant was sharp and would have made an excellent field officer. A shame to lose him this way. The late-afternoon heat begrudgingly yielded to an evening coolness. At least Lieutenant Albright would be partially comfortable. Breed hoped the end would be quick and painless. He chuckled to himself. How can death be painless?

Long, sweeping dark purple and violet shadows enveloped the desert. The multicolored landscape's beauty was magnified in the fading daylight. Blinding yellow sand now reflected a delicate golden light. The fierce red rocks glowed like dying mesquite embers. The desert was hostile and brutal at times, docile and gentle other times. Breed had little difficulty following the patrol. Their hoofprints glared in the sandy riverbed. Breed's mare was a tough gal and could hold a steady gait for what seemed like hours.

As Breed rounded a sharp corner in the serpentine riverbed, he was snapped out of his drifting thoughts by the soft *click* of a hammer being cocked. He stopped, vaguely able to discern the faint outline of a soldier crouching behind a boulder. There was something familiar about the figure. Breed took a gamble. "Will, that you?" he called out. "It's me, Breed."

"Damn, Sarge. I 'bout blasted you." The soldier put his rifle down. "You scared the hell out of me. I wasn't expecting to see you so soon."

"Any problems up ahead?"

"Ya. No-Feet found Indians and is having an argument with that dumb mick. I believe Stills kept Sergeant Fitz from getting killed. How's the lieutenant doing?" Williams expressed his concern for the officer.

"He's dying. I left him as comfortable as possible with a full canteen, rifle, and bedroll." Breed shook his head. "He won't last the night."

"Hell," Will swore bitterly, and chomped down on the toothpick. "With this collection of dudes and sodbusters, we have to leave a man like that behind. It don't seem right." Will spit several pieces of splintered toothpick out.

"I agree, my friend," Breed answered sadly. "Guess I better go save Sergeant Fitz's worthless hide before No-Feet kills him. Keep your eyes and ears open. We could be in for a long night."

Breed prodded the mare. He came into a wide bulge in the riverbed and found the remainder of the patrol. Three men were separated from the main cluster of soldiers. Sergeant Fitz sat in the sand, a bloody handkerchief pressed tight against his bicep. No-Feet squatted on his haunches fifteen feet away, knife in hand. Dave Stills stood squarely between the two. His .45-70 was cocked and leveled. Breed could feel the tension.

"I'll repeat my words," Dave spoke firmly. "The first one who moves, I'll kill." It was an indisputable statement.

The soldiers heard Breed and silently moved apart to let him pass. He slid out of the saddle and quickly appraised the standoff. Breed spoke with authority while looking directly at No-Feet. "Dave, keep an eye on Sergeant Fitz," he instructed. "If he moves, shoot him. Is that perfectly clear? And that goes for Corporal Calhoun also."

"Got it, Breed. Be heedful with No-Feet. He's hair-triggered and ready to go."

Stills turned and faced Sergeant Fitz. His rifle never left the sergeant's chest. Breed gauged the Apache and knew he would kill Fitz or die in an attempt if given half the chance. No-Feet said nothing and slid the knife into his moccasin sheath. Breed gave him wide berth, walked partway down the wash, and waited. No-Feet rose slowly and backed away from Fitz to join Breed. Blue Pine Mesa towered in the foreground as they discussed the best strategy for getting through to the spring.

"How is the spring?"

"Maybe fifteen, twenty braves there. They will leave soon. Later tonight before moonrise we can pass."

Breed left the Indian and walked toward the camp.

Both he and No-Feet were relying on the more or less unspoken practice of leaving a spring open. As he passed the silent soldiers, Breed noticed Sergeant Fitz was being tended to by Corporal Calhoun and Corpsman Perkins. Breed continued on until he found Stills. Dave was sitting beside a riverbed boulder calmly eating his rations. The two soldiers relaxed for the first time all day. "Dave, what in the hell is going on here? We're smack dab in the middle of Apache country and we have a brewing fracas amongst ourselves."

"So you want me to play nursemaid for that hardhead?" Dave smiled at his farfetched suggestion.

"Why don't you?" Breed kidded him, then glanced at the group clustered around Fitz. "On second thought, save yourself the headache. Looks like Fitz has all the help he needs."

"Here's what happened with No-Feet and Fitz. That Apache scouted Blue Pine Mesa. He returned with the news the spring was swarmin' with Indians, and suggested we wait. Fitz got all puffed up like a toad, saying no Injun was going to boss him around." Dave laughed and brushed crumbs from his mustache. "To top that off, Fitz called No-Feet a white man's Injun. No-Feet snatched his knife so fast Fitz didn't have time to blink." Dave tried to keep a straight face but could not. He talked through a splitting grin. "I have to confess I laid a hand on Sergeant Fitz. I knocked him down to keep No-Feet from carving on him. You saw the rest."

"Fitz is too thick-skulled to realize you saved his life. I'll speak with him. When you finish, relieve Williams."

Breed got to his feet and faced Stills. "Thanks for the help." Dave touched the brim of his hat and returned to his meal. As Breed approached Fitz, the group fell silent. "Sergeant Fitz, as soon as the men finish eating I want to talk with them. Muster in about fifteen minutes."

"I'm tellin' you now, Stalwart," Fitz hotly declared, "I'm pressing charges against Stills. Assault and battery on a non-commissioned officer."

"Right, Sergeant Fitz," Breed retorted sharply. "You do that. Overlook the fact he saved your life."

"No doubt you'll smooth things over with your blood brother," Fitz slashed in return.

"I'll fetch him if you want," Breed offered. "You can borrow my knife and settle your differences in the dark. No-Feet would appreciate the opportunity to face you one on one." Breed walked away, then turned. "Fifteen minutes, no more."

"Yes, Sergeant Stalwart. I'll get right on it, Sergeant Stalwart," the big Irishman mimicked with sarcasm. He was "booted and spurred," bolstered by his diehard followers. Fitz knew he got under Breed's skin.

"Those two probably share a peace pipe," Corporal Calhoun said as he jerked his head toward Breed. "They are two of a kind."

"Ya, the same kind. Injun." The men laughed along with Fitz.

• • •

Sergeant Stalwart positioned himself in front of the assembled soldiers. Some knelt, others stood. "Gents, we're in a sorry plight. The spring was occupied earlier. No-Feet is checking it now. We'll await his return. It is vital to refill our canteens and waterbags, and to water the horses. If we can't use the spring tonight, we'll die of thirst startin' tomorrow." The men listened to Breed's explanation. They knew him as an excellent scout and as a man who told his men the facts. "I won't bullshit you. We're in real trouble. When we ride, keep alert and stay awake. Do these things and you *might* live to see another day. Any questions?" No one spoke. There was nothing to say. "One more item which I can't stress enough. Tonight, keep the man ahead of you in close reach. Don't become separated. Tomorrow, stick together. If the Indians split us apart, their job is that much easier. *Stick together!*"

"When's our Injun coming to guide us safely through the night?" Sergeant Fitz asked with mock concern.

"I don't know, Sergeant Fitz. Since you're so preoccupied with his well-being, I'll let you go out and find him." Fitz clammed up. "Finish eating, men. Be ready to ride on short notice. Sergeant, check the men and their gear. No loose cinches or gun loops. No one wear anything that can possible make a noise. Wrap anything metal." Breed rattled out the orders. "It will take one 'clank' and we're dead." Sergeant Fitz continued to sulk but he also knew what Breed had said was true. Their lives depended on stealth and silence.

Breed left the men and found a secluded spot to eat his rations. As he leaned against the warm, smooth face of a boulder, he enjoyed these final minutes of solitude in the fading daylight. Off in the distance he heard a shot, then several more. The shooting came from the direction of Lieutenant Albright. "Give them hell, sir," Breed offered although he knew the outcome.

The lieutenant had waited patiently, yearning to prove himself and to his men he was a good officer and soldier. The Comancheros found three of their horses and rode doubled up. They were pushing their mounts hard trying to catch the patrol. Due to their haste they had become careless, and blundered into Lieutenant Albright's field of fire. The officer drew a bead on the apparent leader, a stocky man, and knocked him brutally out of the saddle. The Mexican's *compañero* sat, shy of belief, on the rump of the horse. That momentary pause cost him his life. Lieutenant Albright drilled him. Pandemonium reigned. The Mexicans scattered like wind-blown chaff.

The lieutenant caught a second rider as his horse bounded over the edge of a shallow gully. The .45-70 slug swept him off the horse with a sickening finality. A cat-and-mouse game followed as the Mexicans steadily tightened their circle around the officer. The Comancheros quickly took advantage of the officer's lack of mobility. One of the Mexicans charged blindly up the slope, his pistols booming out deadly harbingers of death. One of these shots nicked the lieutenant's shoulder and knocked him off his knees. The officer rolled desperately to the right and out of the line of fire. He painfully covered twenty feet on his stomach while he dragged his rifle. He positioned himself beside a small boulder and waited for the gunman. The lieutenant covered more distance than the Mexican anticipated. When the Mexican appeared on the edge of the hill, he was looking away from the officer. Lieutenant Albright fought off the searing pain of both wounds and shot the man; the Comanchero somersaulted off the hill in an avalanche of dust and debris. The officer's shot gave away his position. The remaining Mexicans shot and killed him. The lieutenant died with the knowledge he had succeeded on both his quests.

No-Feet returned with bad news. There were Indian and Comanchero camps on both sides of the approach to Blue Pine Mesa. It would be difficult but not impossible to get to the spring without being seen. Bright moonlight compounded the problem. Breed's decision was not a difficult one. They would press on. There was no other choice. The terrain changed from endless, winding arroyos and canyons to grassy, rolling hills. These sweeping hillocks fanned out from the base of Blue Pine Mesa. The trail the soldiers followed lay deep in the trough of two hills. At present the bottom remained in inky black shadows. The higher ground was splashed in brilliant silvery moonlight.

The patrol gathered around Breed. "Walk your horses from here, but hustle," Breed whispered. "We have to beat the moonlight. No noise! I'll kick the ass off the first man who goofs up," he threatened. "Provided the Indians or Comancheros don't shoot it off first. Move out," he urged them forward.

With No-Feet in the lead, the men marched single-file in the trough bottom. They hugged one side to stay in shadows; a mounted rider would have been bathed in moonlight. Breed was edgy. Every noise seemed magnified. Each sound was the one that would give them away. The file moved briskly and stayed ahead of the relentless creeping light. Breed and Dave lagged behind to protect the rear. Suddenly the men stopped. A horse nickered from above. The men froze where they were. Breed quickly surveyed the moonlit landscape and saw a lone rider on the knoll. He was headed their way. A Comanchero, damn it all to hell, he thought. They will be looking for us all night. The man could not see into the shadows and came down into the trough. If any one of the patrol made the slightest noise, all of them would be trapped. This was not a good site to have to fight out of. Breed's gamble on the Indians not fighting at night seemed to have paid off. But he'd lost with the Mexicans. "We have to get him, Dave," whispered Breed.

"I know. How?"

"When he hits the shadow line, we'll jump him. He won't expect it."

They stealthily turned their horses around and pressed together to avoid the moonlight. Breed would have to mount his mare from the right side. He hoped she would not spook. The Comanchero was twenty yards away and heading directly toward them.

Breed nodded to Stills and simultaneously they mounted. Breed's mare bolted and threw him off. Stills, partially mounted, couldn't get his foot into the stirrup. As Dave raced past the Comanchero, he hurled himself at the man. His leap was short and hit the Mexican mid-thigh. Dave frantically clutched at the Mexican and dragged him off his horse by hanging onto his arm. They fell heavily into the sand. The Mexican landed squarely atop Stills and knocked the wind out of him. The man rolled quickly to his feet and drew his knife. Dave lay stunned and helpless.

Breed lunged frantically at the figure. His bone jarring blow knocked the Mexican head over heels into the sandy river bottom. Breed, stunned by the force of the blow, fell to his knees. He tried to shake the flashing yellow and black kaleidoscope of colors from his head. Dave breathed fitfully and gulped in deep mouthfuls of air. The Mexican had not moved. Breed stood, and with weak knees cautiously approached the prone figure. He toed the man over onto his back. The Mexican had fallen on his own knife.

"That's the first lucky break we've had since we started," Breed commented to Dave.

Dave managed to speak but not without effort. "Let's hope it won't be our last. Wanna dump him in the bushes?" Dave shook sand out of his long hair.

"No, we have to keep moving." Breed walked a short distance down the trough and called softly. "Bancroft?"

"Ja, it's me. Opperman," came the muffled reply from the bulky blacksmith.

"Karl, pass it on. Head for the spring. To hell with the camps. See you there shortly." Breed waited as Karl talked to the man in front of him. Soon the file of soldiers moved down the trough. Breed returned to Stills. "Give me his horse. We'll take it with us."

"I don't have him." Dave quickly searched for the animal. "He probably headed straight back to their camp."

Off in the distance a coyote yipped. Both men froze. They cocked their heads trying to pinpoint its origin. Another yipping. "On the left, where he rode down." Breed pulled his rifle from its scabbard. "That's one of the sickest coyotes I ever heard. Let's check him out."

The two men sprinted up the grassy slope and hunkered down shy of the ridgeline. A glimpse over the rim revealed a campsite tucked in the hollow of the ridge. Three men stood close to a glowing fire. One of them held the reins of the Mexican's horse. A dozen sleeping figures were scattered about the periphery. "Guess that takes care of your good luck, Breed." A smile showed under Dave's bushy mustache.

"Yup. The question is whether they'll wait until sunrise or do something now."

"There's your answer." Dave pointed with his rifle. One man, a gringo, was walking among the sleeping figures, nudging them awake, and talking to them.

"We've gotta get the hell outta here. Let's hide that Mexican in the brush." Breed talked to Dave as they headed for the trough and the body. "I don't know how much time we have." Each grabbed an arm and leg of the dead man and together they heaved him under a droopy weeping willow. Breed kicked sand over the bloody spot in the riverbed.

Dave spoke his suspicions as he swung into the saddle. "There was something familiar about that gringo. I could be mistaken but he looked like Lacy Gantry. I hear tell he's into gun-runnin'."

"I'd need only an hour alone with him and No-Feet. I'd have the answers."

"Invite me along. That's one double-dealin' bastard I would love to get my hands on."

They galloped through the trough and paid no mind to the moonlight. The important matter was to distance themselves from the Comancheros. Breed glanced at their tracks and breathed a deep sigh of relief. Although the night was cool, no moisture had come up from the bed. They weren't leaving any telltale prints.

CHAPTER
5

It was an hour before cockcrow. The tranquil desert was enveloped in a silky pink predawn light. From his vantage point, Walking Tall watched the thirteen-man patrol move slowly toward the plains that footed Twin Buttes. Their progress appeared agonizingly languid; they looked like a centipede from this distance. In a capricious manner nature had made both sides of the buttes impassable. These flanks were deeply cut with towering canyons and sheer rock walls. The natural passage between the two rocky buttes was a gentle rolling sweep.

Walking Tall was a patient man. With forty veteran braves he awaited the arrival of the patrol. The Indians were positioned immediately over the crest of the sweep between the buttes. The younger braves, some armed with repeating rifles, were cocky and spoiling for a fight. Walking Tall had traded fifteen new Winchesters from Campesino. An agreement to help the Mexican Indian was a small price to pay for the new rifles. Campesino and his men had ridden back toward Mexico last night shortly after Breed and Stills discovered their camp.

The previous night's council and war dance had kindled war fever in the braves. Their wizened "Keeper of the Spirits" had spoken of the favorable signs: Spike Buck's sighting of the mountain lion, and the two hawks that accompanied them on their ride here. The spirits of the buttes had spoken to the medicine man and told him it was time to avenge fallen warriors, to shame the white man and scatter his soul.

One quarter of the way up the long sweep lay a deep trench that ran from flank to flank. Bad Limp, with ten braves, was hidden in the left gully. They were to split the patrol. Dog Ears and his ten braves waited in the right gully. These Indians were to circle behind the soldiers and cut off escape to the rear. If the two sub-chieftains succeeded, victory was assured. Walking

Tall sought a swift kill. No-Feet, the white man's eyes and ears, emerged from the trench and began working the sweep in a steady crisscross manner. He was a dead man if he topped the crest. Walking Tall would personally see to it.

Breed sent a flanker in each side of the trench. He instructed them to check thoroughly but not get caught. Private Bancroft slipped into the left gully far enough to escape from Breed's sight. He continued to shirk his responsibilities and had not the slightest intention of going deeper into the gully. If he had gone past the corner, he would have been killed. Bad Limp decided against killing the soldier there. The Indian took a chance on not being discovered. It paid off minutes later.

In the other side of the trench Dog Ears watched as Trooper Williams cautiously checked the gully. He was thorough and good, the Apache noted. The ten braves nudged their ponies out of the gully and over a gentle crest in order to circle behind the patrol. By the time Williams spotted these tracks the patrol was trapped.

Breed waited for the men to report back before proceeding further. Private Bancroft trotted back into sight and reined in beside Breed. Too quick, thought Breed.

"Nothing there, Sergeant Stalwart," the private reported.

"How far did you check?" Breed questioned the recalcitrant soldier. Bancroft groped for an answer. "Damn it, man. How far did you go?" Breed raked him for a reply. "Your scalp depends on it."

"Pretty far," he lied. "I rode fast."

Breed looked him in the eye, then glanced at his rested pony. Bancroft knew he had been caught. Breed pointed toward the gully but a shout cut him short of sending Bancroft for a second time. Williams thundered out of his side of the gully, his horse running at a furious pace. He slid to a stop next to Breed.

"Ten, maybe twelve sets of tracks up that gully. I think we've been had." Williams cast a fearful glance behind the patrol. "They've circled us."

A chorus of shouts and yips came from behind the patrol. Breed looked back and saw Dog Ears and his braves bearing down on them. Escape to the rear was denied the soldiers. Breed yelled to his men, "Go up the other gully." He headed for the left side.

"No," screamed Bancroft. "I didn't clear it." Panic and shame etched his face. The words had no sooner left his mouth than Bad Limp and his braves thundered out of the gully.

The patrol stampeded from the trench onto the sweep. The more experienced horsemen moved ahead. Trooper Glade, the slow-witted Reb, and Corpsman Perkins predictably lagged behind. Bad Limp wouldn't split the patrol as planned, but joined Dog Ears in sealing off escape. Karl Opperman, the hulking smithy, and the retarded Private Hinton rode wherever their horses took them.

Breed lunged ahead. "Stay together," he yelled, and pointed toward the right butte as he tried to get his men to follow. The general flow was headed in that direction when Walking Tall struck. The warriors surged over the crest. Their charge would have been the envy of any U.S. Cavalry commander. In a picture perfect wedge they split the patrol. The complete lack of resistance from the soldiers confused the Indians as their charge carried them through the patrol. It was a free-for-all. Every man for himself.

Private Bancroft paid dearly for his lackluster attitude and careless scouting. He had been slow to ride out of the trench and was the last man. The Indians felt victory as they viciously competed for first coup against the soldiers. Bancroft glanced over his shoulder and saw the braves gain on him. He knew he was a goner and cried out for help. Private Loppitt, the still-defiant Confederate, heard Bancroft's call and looked around. Loppitt half turned in his saddle, raised his rifle, and shot Strong Legs off his pony. Loppitt flipped open the breech and reloaded. He searched for Bancroft but could not find him.

The Apaches had overtaken Private Bancroft and competed for first coup. Talks True and Half Moon Up hit Bancroft at the same time. Talks True smashed the soldier's spine with a stone coup club as Half Moon Up buried his coup stick deep into the soldier's skull. Bancroft fell from his mount. Spotted Fox lanced the downed soldier, skewering him to the ground. Loppitt, a natural with a rifle, aimed through the dust and shot at Spotted Fox. Although he thought he hit the brave, Spotted Fox rode away yipping victoriously at his kill. Talks True and Half Moon Up circled Bancroft's body in celebration of the first coup.

Corpsman Perkins and Trooper Glade were doomed because of their poor riding abilities. Together they veered out of control toward Walking Tall's massed braves. Perkins was hopelessly tangled in the canvas strap of his medical bag and couldn't get to his pistol. All he could do was hang on. Perkins's inexperience and reckless charge carried him in front of the braves. He never had a chance. His bullet-riddled and pin-cushioned body thudded to the grass. Prairie Hawk rode to the body and shot an arrow through the corpsman's chest, thus laying coup to him.

Trooper Glade, slow to react, at least had the presence of mind to defend himself. He snapped off an aimless shot at the braves. His bullet hit Three Fingers in the forehead, killing him instantly. Rut slipped under the neck of his pony and shot an arrow from his stubby mulberry bow. Glade was hit under the rib cage and slammed to the ground. He desperately scrambled to his feet, but Dark Like A Shadow raced past and split his skull with a coup stick.

In the ensuing mayhem Breed, No-Feet, Corporal Calhoun, Sergeant Fitz, and Stills rode for and reached the foot of the right butte. Corporal Calhoun and Sergeant Fitz both had flesh wounds but were capable of fighting. These five men used the boulders for defensive positions and laid down deadly accurate fire. The Indians were reluctant to charge them. The other five troopers, the marksman Loppitt, dimwitted Private Hinton, smithy Opperman, the guidon bearer Cara-binieri, and Williams struggled for the left butte. As

Carabinieri rode for the safety of the boulders, two braves charged to head him off. Instinctively the Italian dipped the guidon shaft to a horizontal attitude and speared Contrary squarely in the chest. The wooden carved eagle on the top of the staff splintered into the Indian and killed him as it propelled him off his pony. The second brave, Long Knife, lived up to his name. He swerved close to the soldier and slashed savagely with his knife. He cut the guidon bearer from shoulder to hip. Long Knife raised his bloodied weapon in a salute and yipped in victory. His bravado cost him. Williams's shot slammed him from his pony onto the ground. He Who Fears Nothing swooped down and picked up the wounded brave. Together they rode away from the soldiers.

A bloodbath of mutilation on the grassy field came to an end. The Indians disfigured the dead soldiers many times over. The soldiers were flayed, with strips of skin ripped from their bodies. The Indians shot countless arrows into the soldiers' bodies. As a final insult the Indians tied the corpses behind their ponies and dragged them up the sweep. This show of disrespect and contempt was done to bait the soldiers. Opperman, not accustomed to this brutality as a blacksmith, lost his nerve and shot ineffectually at the Indians. Private Hinton, also unnerved and not knowing any better, joined in.

"Stop shooting, you fools," Williams shouted in frustration. "That's exactly what they want, for you to lose your heads and waste ammo." Will settled down and took command of the four soldiers. He had been in difficult positions before and was no stranger to being in charge.

"You want me to show you how it's done?" Loppitt asked Will, a smile on his young face.

"Can you drop one?" Will queried as he shifted the toothpick from one side of his mouth to the other.

"Ah, man," Loppitt complained. "My daddy would whop my ass if I couldn't drop one of them Indians from here. I could do it with my eyeballs half shut."

"Do it," Will told him.

The braves doubled back. This time they rode slowly past the boulders with total contempt for the white men. As they drew abreast, Loppitt rested his rifle on the flat surface of the rock. He glanced up, gauged once, then shot. The noise of the solitary shot thundered off Twin Buttes. Mas o Menos, a half-breed, bounced off the grass. The other braves whipped their ponies out of rifle range.

"I take it that's what you had in mind." Loppitt smiled at Will. "One less Indian to worry about."

"Nice shot, Loppitt." Will congratulated the Georgian. "I think all you did was piss off a whole lot of Indians."

Williams was faced with two choices. He could stay close to the grass and keep the Indians out of the boulders. And risk being overrun. His other choice was to fall back into the boulders and fight from better positions. With Carabinieri badly wounded, Will chose the boulders. The Italian was sheltered in the shade of a huge boulder. He was in great pain and losing blood despite the bandages Will had applied.

Breed and Stills watched Loppitt's sniping with mixed emotions. Stills was the first to break the silence. "That, my friend," the hardened trooper noted, "is going to cost us dearly." The trooper pulled at the corners of his mustache.

"Sure is, Dave. But damned if that lad can't shoot. I wish Williams had several more like him." Breed cupped his hands and hollered across the gap between the two buttes. His voice rebounded off the cliffs. "Will, can you hear me?" Williams waved in reply. "If you get attacked first, keep the Indians out of the boulders. Don't let them get a foothold or you're done. We'll try and help you out."

"We'll do our best, Sarge." Will yelled. "If you are first, we'll lend a hand."

The ten troopers made ready for the pending attack. The Indians began a game of nerves. They sent out riders to test the responses of the soldiers. Several times during the morning they showed themselves, massed, and made ready to attack. They feinted several times then disappeared. These maneuvers succeeded in unsettling some of the soldiers, making them more edgy.

The day dragged on. No contact had been made for several hours. The soldiers baked in the sun, precious little shade to be found. On Williams's side of the buttes, Carabinieri was in bad shape. Will had made a shelter out of his blanket and in the shade he gently helped the Italian sip water. Carabinieri had refused to surrender either the guidon or flag and clutched both next to his side. Any movement opened his wound, and he had lost a considerable amount of blood. Will looked across to Breed's side of the buttes. The fierce heat distorted shapes and the landscape simmered as he tried to see what was happening.

Sergeant Fitz asked Corporal Calhoun to fetch him some water. The corporal's temper was as hot as the day. "I'm sick and tired of being your boy. Yes, Sergeant Fitz. No, Sergeant Fitz," Calhoun shouted as he rose to his feet. "I want no more of your army life."

"I'm still in charge of you, Corporal. Don't you forget it," Fitz snapped back. His thigh wound hurt like hell and he didn't feel like arguing with the pop-off corporal.

"You ain't in charge of shit," retorted Calhoun.

"That's right, boy. Long as I have people like you, I ain't in charge of shit."

"Get off my back, Sarge, or I'll . . ."

"Or you'll what, boy?"

Breed stepped between the men and spoke to both of them. "Let's forget this whole—"

"The hell with—" was all Corporal Calhoun spit out before Breed decked him. Breed reached down, grabbed both shirt lapels, and yanked Calhoun into the air.

"I won't repeat this. Enough! You understand?" Corporal Calhoun blinked in fear. It was hard to argue with a man who was holding you six inches off the ground while showing no signs of strain. The corporal meekly nodded. Breed set his feet onto mother earth.

"Here they come, Breed," Stills calmly called. "They look serious this time." Dave Stills carefully placed six extra rounds on the rock in front of him.

A familiar hair-raising feeling inched up the back of Breed's neck. His stomach knotted with the dread gut feeling of death. He couldn't keep those feelings away. His palms were wet and clammy. The Indians over-flowed the trench as they assembled on the sweep. Walking Tall was in the middle, Dog Ears and Bad Limp on either side. The lesser hierarchy filled out the front row with ten braves abreast. It was difficult to see, but there appeared to be three full rows behind the front row.

"Oh, man," Breed muttered, "are we in trouble now. "With those Winchesters up front, we'll be fortunate to leave here with our hair." Breed's men wormed deeper into their defensive positions.

On the other side Williams spoke with each of his men. He knew what was about to take place. "Alfredo, you awake?" Will asked the Italian as he removed the flags from the man's hand and leaned them against a rock. The guidon bearer opened his eyes a slit then nodded weakly. "Good. Take your .45 and shoot anyone who comes over those boulders." Will pointed them out to him. "You're our last hope. Can you do it?"

"*Sì,* Señore Will. I can do it," he gamely replied as he searched for the flags, then spotted them by the rock.

"The honor of those flags is mine. Let me have them, I beg of you. They must be safe with me."

"You're on," Will reassured him. "Loppitt, give the flags to Private Carabinieri." The gesture alleviated the Italian's fears. Will suspected Carabinieri knew this was the end. Williams moved down the line and stopped to talk with the slow-witted Private Hinton, and Karl Opperman, blacksmith turned soldier. "Hinton, if you want to stay alive, do your damnedest to keep the Indians out of the boulders." Will looked for an indication he was getting through. "Shoot their ponies but don't let them get in." Will knew for a fact Hinton didn't have the faintest idea of the grim outlook of the pending battle.

"Karl, come over here next to Hinton. Cover this area." Will swept his hand to show Karl where he meant. Karl forced himself behind a small boulder and moved it slightly forward to accommodate his bulk. Williams noticed neither soldier had spare rounds out. "I'll show you a quick way to get off four shots." Will reached into his cartridge belt and removed three rounds. He stuck them between the last three fingers of his left hand. "Now look. Cradle your rifle between your thumb and index finger, resting the weight in the palm of your hand. Reload by taking a shell out from between your fingers." Will deftly plucked the shells out to demonstrate his method. "Four fast shots. Make them count, your lives depend on it. Either of you have any questions?"

Neither man spoke. Will knew these two were the

weak links in his defenses. He would have to watch them carefully and be ready to help out if a critical situation arose. He worked his way to Loppitt. "No need to tell you anything. I'm counting on you, Loppitt."

The lanky Georgian smiled. "Don't put the shuck on me, Will. I know we ain't leavin' here alive."

"You're probably right, Loppitt." Will rested his hand on the lad's shoulder. "By damn we'll make them pay for it. Keep an eye on those two." Will pointed with his toothpick in the direction of Opperman and Hinton. "They'll need divine guidance to get out of this mess."

Loppitt appeared resigned to the circumstances beyond his control. He laughed and reflected seriously on his thoughts. One of his grandfather's sayings came to mind. Some days you get the bear, some days the bear gets you. "Well, Grandpap, today the bear gets me." Loppitt took on a determined tone. He remembered back on his war experience. "I surrendered once, with General Lee. I don't have any intention of doing it again."

The Indians were several hundred yards away. Walking Tall and the front row eased into a gentle trot. The other ranks followed the pace. Soon they broke into a full gallop, yipping and yelling in earnest. The first two rows swerved violently toward Will and his four soldiers. The repeating rifles fired first. Will was doomed. Through a withering hail of lead, wildly ricocheting bullets, and splintering rock, Will and Loppitt held their sector. They knocked down several front-line braves and ponies. Even so the charge succeeded. The Indians leapt from their thundering ponies and slipped into the boulder field. Ineffective fire from Opperman and Hinton opened up their flank. Loppitt saw what was happening and scrambled over the boulders to their positions. Hinton was shooting furiously and hitting nothing.

"Slow down, Hinton," Loppitt yelled at him. "Take your time. Choose your target."

"They're too many." He was panicky. "What'll we do?"

"Pick out one particular Indian and pop him," Loppitt casually instructed as he dropped a charging brave at the foot of the boulders.

"But they're already in the rocks," the private cried out with fear cracking his voice.

"No problem," Loppitt commented. "Watch where he goes in. Take a gamble he'll come out again from the same place." Loppitt calmly sighted on a large gray boulder forty yards downhill. As Hinton watched, an Indian bolted from behind the rock and the Georgian fired. The big slug caught the Indian broadside and knocked him between the boulders. "Just like that." Loppitt smiled. "Now get shootin'."

Opperman was struggling to undo a jammed cartridge, his thick fingers hindering the delicate task. Every second he lost gave the Indians that much more of an advantage in the boulder field. Loppitt quickly snapped off a shot at an advancing Indian. He missed. "Goddlemighty, Loppitt," he cursed himself, "slow down. Opperman, get the hell shootin'," Loppitt yelled back at Opperman. "We're losing ground in a hurry. Opperman?"

No answer from the trooper. Loppitt glanced around at the blacksmith. Opperman was dead, slumped over his rifle with an arrow protruding between his shoulder blades. Instinct told Loppitt to move. He lunged to his left, dodging between two boulders. An arrow splintered against the rock where he stood moments before. "Why, you cocky son of a gun," he remarked to his Indian opponent.

Loppitt searched and saw the Indian standing in front of a large flat slab. He was notching another arrow. Loppitt struggled to bring the rifle to his shoulder but knew he had acted too late. As if in slow motion, he watched the arrow come toward him. A sledgehammer blow knocked his right leg out from beneath him. His rifle discharged against the boulder in front of him, spraying rock splinters and lead in all directions. The arrow had hit Loppitt in the thigh and lodged at an upward angle into his right buttock. His resulting fall snapped the shaft. The right side of his body screamed out in burning, searing pain. He was stunned. With watery eyes he watched helplessly as the Indian drew back another arrow. A thunderous crack of a rifle sent the brave slamming into the slab. The Indian slowly slid to the dirt. Loppitt looked around and saw Private Hinton smiling his wide, dumb grin.

"Thanks, Hinton," he choked out.

A small pebble bounced off the boulder beside Private Hinton but he paid it no mind. He should have. It was a measuring rock thrown off the top of the butte. From the flat surface of the boulder upon which he lay, Loppitt rolled over onto his back. In this manner he could slide his dead leg. The move allowed him to see the Indian on top of the butte lift a rock above his head and hurl it down. Loppitt bit through his lip fighting back pain as he raised his rifle and shot the Indian. The brave twisted in a pirouette and pitched off the cliff. His body fell swiftly and landed with a meaty thud amongst the boulders. The rock he had thrown smashed Hinton in the middle of the back and pounded him underneath a boulder. Loppitt attempted to pull himself off the exposed surface. He didn't make it. The volume of fire intensified and he died there, hit by four bullets and two more arrows.

Williams witnessed his troopers die and knew he was next. I'll take a few with me, he issued the challenge. He waited with fatal resignation. It didn't take the Indians long to exploit the situation. Will used his cunning and deadly determination to kill Still Water and Bear Claw. He shot them both as they approached the boulders. Bull Elk jumped Will as he reloaded, but the trooper managed to club him unconscious with his rifle butt. A bullet creased Will's side and another nicked his shoulder. Walking Tall had taken both shots at Will but could not hit the elusive soldier.

Dropping further into the boulders Will found his place. He pulled his .45 and waited. Four braves crouched by the large boulder that fronted him. On a given signal they charged the cornered trooper. Dog Ears and Coup went over the top. The other braves, Bad Limp and Wind-That-Bodes-Ill, circled the boulder. Williams shot and killed Dog Ears and hit Bad Limp with two well-placed shots. Wind-That-Bodes-Ill clubbed the pistol from Will's hand, breaking the trooper's wrist in the process. Coup hit Will a smashing blow to the head which knocked him out cold. The braves pounced on him in cold-blooded glee. A captive was the culmination of a successful battle.

Trooper Alfredo Carabinieri waited. He reminisced about the day he became an American citizen and about his cavalry training. He was the best damned bugler and guidon bearer that Fort McHenry had ever seen. Carabinieri had been overlooked because he was out of the action. The bloody orgy began as the Indians butchered and mutilated the soldiers. El Niño crept toward the Italian trooper thinking he was dead. Carabinieri quickly raised his pistol and shot him in the chest. The deafening shot startled the Indians, who scattered for cover. Antelope mistakenly ran past the Italian. Carabinieri killed him there. Long Knife sprinted toward the trooper, his knife pointed at Carabinieri's heart. The soldier took his revenge. His first shot hit the Indian in the hip and knocked him off his feet. As Long Knife struggled to his knees, Carabinieri shot him again. The brave was bowled over and slammed against a rock. Long Knife managed to lift his hand as if to throw his knife. The third of Carabinieri's shots snuffed out his life. Carabinieri calmly put the pistol barrel against his right temple and pulled the trigger.

The Indians were outraged. A wounded soldier had taken three of their best braves and cheated them by death. They fell upon him with a special vengeance. The Indians recalled the words of the "Keeper of the Spirits." Victory was theirs.

Sergeant Fitz's Irish luck seemed to have held for the soldiers. The Indians who attacked Breed and his troopers weren't properly led and had chosen the toughest of the lot. Their attack was more for show, to make the soldiers defend themselves. Unlike Walking Tall and his braves, these Indians did not get off the first shots. Breed's troopers knocked down half the front row with their initial volley. When the Indians failed to reach the boulders they quickly joined the carnage on the other side. Walking Tall's braves had gained the boulder field so quickly on Will's side, Breed and his men were afraid to shoot for fear of hitting a soldier. The fight was bloody, violent, and finished quickly. The troopers watched in stunned disbelief at the unmitigated brutality.

"Where's Williams?" Breed asked. "Did anyone see him go down?"

A sickening fear hit the soldiers. The worst had happened to one of their own. Capture. To kill yourself was better than to fall into the hands of the Apaches. Brave, fearless men had pulled their own triggers to avoid capture. As the troopers watched, two braves dragged Will out of the boulders and paraded him toward Walking Tall and the other mounted Indians.

"Shoot him," Breed pleaded. "For God's sake, shoot him."

Stills was kneeling behind a boulder dressing a shallow wound in his forearm. No-Feet had gone to the horses to make ready for a possible escape attempt. Sergeant Fitz and Corporal Calhoun watched but did nothing. Breed bolted to them and yanked the rifle out of Calhoun's hand. He quickly shouldered the rifle and rested it on top of a boulder. He drew in a deep breath, held steady on Williams, and shot. Breed quickly pulled another shell from his cartridge belt, loaded flawlessly, and without hesitation shot Will again. The first echo was rebounding from the cliffs when Breed shot for the second time. The Indians dropped Williams's body to the ground. Breed had hit Will with both shots.

Outraged at the loss of their live captive, Rump and Brother-of-the-Weasel impaled Will's body on the broken shaft of a lance. He was immediately riddled with dozens of arrows. A chorus of war cries and victory yelps filled the air. Now to finish the battle by killing the remaining white men.

Breed discarded the rifle and sought solitude in the boulders. In gut-wrenching spasms he threw up. Tears streaked his face as he silently grieved for Will Williams. Stills had watched the incident and breathed a silent prayer for his fallen partner. He admired Breed for his courage and hoped if Will's plight ever befell him, someone would do the same. No-Feet watched the shooting. He felt no emotion for the dead white man. His only feelings were that Breed would have made a good Indian. Sergeant Fitz and Corporal Calhoun were talking in hushed whispers about the shooting.

Breed fought to regain his composure. He returned to his position ready for the pending attack. No one spoke. The troopers concentrated as the Indians massed at the southern end of the grassy field. Walking Tall, along with his newly elevated subchiefs, Coup and Rut, squatted on their haunches in a tight circle.

"You see what's going on there, lads," Breed spoke, his voice cracking but gaining strength. "The next charge will determine who rides out and who rots here in the sun." The soldiers were ready. Each man checked and rechecked his rifle for the hundredth time. Spare ammo was laid out and .45's were rechecked and holstered. The men realized the stacked odds, yet faced them with strength of mind. Their fear didn't show.

The Indians broke from the talks and mounted. Their numbers appeared to cover the sweep. Walking Tall took his position in the middle, flanked by Coup and Rut. The lesser braves in the pecking order filled out either side. The Indians moved forward in a slow trot. The soldiers were seeing a repeat performance of that morning's charge.

As Walking Tall lifted his arm to signal the charge, a solitary shot sounded from the trench. A single Indian rider raced from the mouth of the trench and hurtled onto the grassy field. Walking Tall held his braves in check. The stocky pony ate up the distance between the Indians. The leaders separated themselves from the front rank, off-horsed, and waited. The lathered pony skidded to a halt as the rider leapt to the ground and joined them.

For several minutes the Indians talked, sometimes with heated discussion. Coup was furious, jumped to his feet, and angrily pointed at the soldiers. Walking Tall, still squatting, silenced him with a wave of his hand. The debate continued with the four Indians glancing occasionally toward the soldiers. The council ended abruptly. Walking Tall stood and mounted his pony. The others followed with the exception of Coup, who was still fuming mad. Walking Tall had spoken and Coup wasn't buying it. The chief, his patience worn thin, motioned the brave to mount. Coup did so but with visible reluctance.

The front row of Indians began to ride slowly toward the soldiers. Five hammers cocked as one. "Easy, boys." Breed spoke calmly. "Let them get a little closer."

Within seventy yards of the soldiers Walking Tall heel-flanked his pony away from the troopers and headed off the sweep. The other braves followed him. One loud sigh escaped from the mouths of the soldiers.

"What in the hell?" Sergeant Fitz asked, completely perplexed by the Indian's behavior.

"No one move and for damned sure don't shoot," Breed implored. "We've been saved by that rider. I don't know why."

"I can't believe it, Sarge." Calhoun asked Fitz, "What are they doing?" Fitz said nothing and shrugged his shoulders.

"We've been scorned by the Indians," Breed told him. "They didn't feel we were worth the trouble of killing. They had us and knew it."

"I'm glad that one hoppin'-mad Indian wasn't in charge," Dave uttered as he ran fingers through his hair, "or we would have been here for the duration."

Breed was still dumbfounded over the sudden departure of Walking Tall and his braves. "I can't imagine what was so important for them to abandon the fight. It saved our scalps." The soldiers watched as the Indians crossed the trench and turned into the vast desert. They vanished like a mirage.

"Let's not dally, men. Sergeant Fitz, take Corporal Calhoun and see if you can find any of Will's horses. Then get our men out of the boulders. We'll bury them here. Stills and I will find the others."

No-Feet brought the horses out of the boulders. The men mounted and headed in their respective directions. Breed and Stills searched the western gully first. They found nothing. A search of the other gully revealed the three soldiers killed in the initial fight. It was difficult to comprehend the Indian's excessive brutality toward the soldiers. Breed and Stills were sickened. They suppressed the strong desire to turn and ride away. "We'll bury them here, Dave. It will be easier in the sandy river bottom."

The two men scraped a waist-deep grave in the sand.

They worked fast and sweated heavily in the heat. Breed used blankets to wrap the soldiers. They were laid gently in the common grave. It was a grisly task. Breed scrounged through the mesquite trees and found enough limbs to partially cover the bodies. The mesquite was weighed down with heavy rocks. Breed and Stills filled in the grave before they rode their horses over the top of it. When they finished, the grave blended in perfectly with the river bottom. Nearly a half hour later they rode out of the trench and joined Sergeant Fitz and Corporal Calhoun at the edge of the boulder field. Five blanket-wrapped bodies lay on the grass.

"No horses, Breed. Injuns must have run them off. We brung them bodies down here."

"Thanks, Sergeant. Let's bury them. Find a shallow ditch or hole. It'll save digging."

After a brief search a natural dip was found between two huge boulders. The five soldiers were buried side by side. A thin layer of rock covered them. The troopers scraped and pushed dirt over the grave with their bare hands. Breed walked the horses back and forth over the grave to pack the dirt and to blend it in with the torn and scarred field.

"Why are you doing that?" Corporal Calhoun asked, aghast at the thought of desecrating a grave.

"This way we protect the bodies from scavenging animals and angry Indians," Stills explained.

"But why?" Corporal Calhoun still didn't understand.

"The Indians believe if a body is mutilated here in present life, the soul will be similarly mutilated in future life. It is also a scare tactic. If you tear a body badly enough, people will think twice about nosing about," Dave said patiently, filling Calhoun in on the reasoning behind Breed's actions.

"Oh," was all Calhoun said.

"Gentlemen, I suggest we ride like hell away from here while we still can," Breed told his soldiers as he swung into his saddle.

"Sergeant Stalwart." Corporal Calhoun handed Breed the flag and guidon. "We found them by Carabinieri. The Indians trampled and tore them all to hell."

Breed tied the swallowtailed cavalry guidon and the blue-and-yellow regimental flag behind the cantle. The broken shafts stuck out, splintered ends and ragged cloth mute testimony to the Indians' fury. Here are your colors, Colonel Prentice. For whatever the hell they are worth. Breed felt an angry wrath deep inside.

The five survivors rode from the hidden grave site in stoney silence. No one spoke but each man thought about his fallen comrades. All felt the loss yet each shared an unspoken relief of survival as they distanced themselves from the Twin Buttes of death. The threat of Walking Tall and his braves made the return trip grueling and tension-filled.

CHAPTER
6

As the survivors of the decimated Twin Buttes patrol rode onto the mesa, they could see furious activity among the sentries in Fort Manning. Their arrival had been announced. The heavy log gates opened for them. Breed untied the flag and guidon, unfurled them, and rested the broken shafts against his thigh. The tattered remnants fluttered pathetically in the breeze. Here were the colors Colonel Prentice wanted shown to the Apache nation. The five survivors fell in a line abreast and trotted proudly and somewhat defiantly through the main gate. There were no cheers or shouted greetings. Silent knowing looks welcomed the soldiers back. The culled patrol continued across the parade grounds and halted in front of the commanding officer's tie rail. A nervous, foot-shifting private was posted by the front door. Breed spoke to him. "Private, would you please inform Colonel Prentice the Twin Buttes patrol has returned and is reporting as ordered."

The private, unsure of what to expect from Breed, spoke softly. "Sergeant Stalwart, Colonel Prentice left orders he was not to be disturbed until further notice. He wants your report first thing in the morning."

Breed listened in disbelief, refusing to believe what he heard. His temper flared, his face flushed crimson. He threw both flag and guidon at the unsuspecting private in angry disgust. The soldier caught them out of self-preservation and stepped back in startled dismay. "When the good colonel is available, would you give him those flags? They tell the story."

Breed brought his anger under rein. He fought the impulse to storm into the colonel's office and demand an answer from the man. How did Colonel Prentice feel, knowing nine men died to satisfy his ego? The cost had been too great and not a damn blasted thing had been accomplished. Breed wheeled his mare violently around and spurred her hard in an attempt to get away as fast as possible. No-Feet and the others followed. None of the soldiers had uttered a word. If one of them had suddenly looked back, he would have seen the colonel peeking from his office window. No one was more relieved to see the soldiers ride away than Colonel Prentice. He'd heard every word. He would not have to face them until tomorrow morning. By then he would know the facts. His gamble on the success of the patrol had died with those troopers and he knew it.

Colonel Prentice waited for the last soldier to disappear from view before he cracked his office door. "Private, get in here," he growled. After the young man was inside, the officer threatened him. "If you ever want to see your home and family again, listen up. Find Sergeant Fitz while he is alone. Alone!" The officer slammed his fist on the desktop to emphasize the point. "Tell him I want to see him as soon as possible and without fanfare. Understand?"

"Yes, sir. Alone and no fuss, sir."

"Inform him I'll wait as long as necessary but I must

see him before tomorrow. Now get out of here." The private saluted and was waved out of the room. "Damn it all to hell," the colonel swore angrily. "Something stupid happened out there. It was their fault, not mine. I was firmly in command here." Colonel Prentice talked to himself, convinced he had acted properly. "I will not tolerate insubordination nor will I be held responsible for some mother's-milk lieutenant and his war-college tactics."

The five survivors enjoyed their first cooked meal in days. The fresh venison was juicy and tender, thick gravy smothered the spuds, and the sweet corn was delicious. All of this was washed down with stout, black coffee. No-Feet was afloat with a half-dozen cups of sugar-flavored coffee. After the meal, Breed and Stills were able to loosen up and talk about the abortive reconnoiter with a select few of the old-timers. The consensus of opinion had the patrol doomed to failure from its inception. The veterans fully understood the futility of the mission, and harbored bitter feelings at the return of so few of their fellow soldiers. Long after the others had turned in, Breed finished his report and asked the messenger of the watch to deliver it to Colonel Prentice. Breed went to bed and slept soundly for the first time since the patrol departed.

Private Riley, the messenger of the watch, rapped on the commanding officer's door and was hailed inside. He snapped a crisp salute to the colonel. "Private Riley with Sergeant Stalwart's report, sir."

"Thank you, private," Colonel Prentice replied with a casual wave. "I accept this report with great anticipation." He laughed loudly as he took the papers. The private backed away from the colonel and the accompanying strong smell of whiskey.

"Night, sir." He saluted again and exited in haste. As Private Riley turned from the closed door, he bumped into Sergeant Fitz. " 'Scuse me, Sergeant Fitz. I didn't see you in the shadows."

"You're right, private," Fitz answered awkwardly, then threateningly. "You didn't see me."

The private knew all too well how to play the game. "No, Sarge. I didn't see nothin'."

The soldier hustled from the porch as if not wanting Fitz's crooked ways to rub off on him. Fitz swore under-breath at this ill-timed encounter. He knocked softly on the door.

"Come in," boomed the colonel's loud voice. Fitz shrugged, dreading what was in store for the next several hours. He shouldered the door open and stepped quickly inside. The commanding officer was slouched in his leather chair, whiskey bottle cradled in his hand. "Ah, the top of the mornin' to you, Shamus Fitzpatrick. Or whatever the hell time of day or night it is. Were you carrying your lucky shamrock on the patrol?" Colonel Prentice asked the question with a thick Irish brogue. "Have a nip of some fine Irish whiskey." It was a statement, not a question.

"Thank you, sir. It would be my pleasure." Fitz poured half a glass then sat.

"Now, Sergeant Fitz. Why don't you tell me every little detail about the patrol and I do mean every detail." The colonel propped both feet on the desktop. He downed his drink in one pull and sat waiting.

Private Riley, standing double watch that night, would be on duty until 0400. After midnight he saw Sergeant Fitz leave the colonel's office. The sergeant was having difficulty walking. Riley had seen Fitz drunk before and made himself scarce. The private knew tomorrow's duty section was in for sheer hell with Fitz drunk at this late hour. "Nope, General Fitzpatrick"—Riley smiled—"I didn't see nothin', sir."

Colonel Prentice was sober enough to realize Fitz still had him pinned between a rock and a hard place. How was he going to get out of this predicament? He slammed his fist in his palm out of frustration. The colonel stood, then fell heavily against his desk and tumbled to the floor. He was too drunk to stand. He pushed himself to his knees and cursed out loud. "Damn you, Major General Ambrose Everett Burnside," he muttered bitterly. "The plague on Fredericksburg and the whole damn war between the blue and gray."

Memories of the Civil War flashed through Colonel Prentice's head. Memories he tried to suppress. December 11 through December 15, 1862. The Union chain of command with names and faces he knew: Generals Burnside, William Buel Franklin, and George Meade. The men he'd fought beside: Crouch, Zook,

French, and Hancock. These soldiers were fresh in his memory.

The battle of Marye's Heights. This hill overlooked the town of Fredericksburg and the Rappahannock River. The Confederate Army of North Carolina, sheltered behind a stone wall, held the heights. The Union Army, under the command of General Franklin, attempted to take the strategic heights that dominated the countryside. French's division was pinned down while being mercilessly cut to shreds. Hancock ordered Zook's brigade forward. They battled to within twenty-five yards of the rebels fighting from behind the stone wall. Their losses were staggering. French lost 1169, Hancock even more: 2037. A young Captain Prentice had thirty men under his immediate command that morning when he marched with French. After the first charge up the heights, Captain Prentice had seven survivors left with him. By midday the captain fought under Zook.

By now Colonel Prentice was wholly absorbed in the past. He shouted vacantly. "Don't go up onto the heights. You'll be killed. That wall can't be taken." Panic laced his voice. "I'm getting out of here. I don't want to die on this hill."

Vivid recollections were relived. Captain Prentice had thrown his worthless saber to the ground and run from that death hill. He had run past the Irish Brigade and Caldwell's troops marching toward the front. To hell with them, he thought. They will all die there. Captain Prentice ran until exhaustion felled him. He crossed the railroad tracks that led into Fredericksburg proper. For two days he hid in an abandoned feed storage warehouse, an AWOL officer. On the third day of the battle the bluecoats abandoned the fight for Marye's Heights. The Johnny Rebs held the heights, waved their damned Confederate flags, and yelled until Captain Prentice wanted to tear his eyes out and plug his ears.

On the night of December 15, 1862, the Army of the Potomac crossed the Rappahannock River in defeat. They had been soundly defeated by the Confederate Army of North Carolina. The Union's losses of dead, wounded, and missing totaled 12,653.

"Yes, sir," a drunken Colonel Prentice spoke to his phantom audience as he poured another drink. "That battle cost two good soldiers their careers. General Burnside was relieved by General Hooker. General Franklin resigned his commission." With crystal clarity, Colonel Prentice continued to relive the battle of Fredericksburg. He remembered tearing up his orders from Zook and stripping his chevrons from his uniform. He stuffed everything between a crack in the busted floor of the warehouse. He left his shameful past there.

The number of Union stragglers was overwhelming and Captain Prentice mingled in with the flood of blue. He rejoined his command in the rear and stated he'd fought until there was no one left. Captain Prentice's commanding officer accepted his word without question. "All the time I knew I was a liar and a coward. I had abandoned my command, my fellow soldiers. Oh, my God. I'm so ashamed," the wretched man cried out in despair.

With the whiskey in control, Colonel Prentice wept openly. He was in his own private hell. His shame drove him with unleashed fury and made him a desperate, irrational man. The immediate field promotion to major after Fredericksburg for "gallantry and bravery above and beyond the call of duty" was the crowning insult to his disgrace. Every time he had been addressed as Major Prentice it was salting an open, festering wound.

The colonel glanced through Breed's report and felt a welling dislike for the man. He feared Breed and sensed the soldier was waiting for the opportunity to discredit him. Colonel Prentice also harbored a grudging admiration for the scout, his self-confidence, manner, and pride in duty.

While making his rounds, Private Riley heard the colonel shouting and carrying on. Suddenly the ranting discourse was cut short by a loud crash of breaking furniture. On his own Private Riley headed for officers' row. The officers' dependents were housed in a separate area within the grounds. This complex was removed from the mainstream life of the fort. Colonel Prentice lived in one of the small cottages. The colonel's daughter, Josephine, shared the living quarters. Private Riley roused the live-in maid and explained the situation to her. Within fifteen minutes Josie Prentice was escorted to her father's office.

Josie quietly slipped inside the office and leaned against the door, and closed it without a noise. She was tall, five feet eight inches, filly-legged as her father said, and blessed with a perky temperament. She had inherited her mother's beauty and grace. At twenty Josie was a strikingly beautiful, full-figured young woman. She spent the last two years in Kansas City at Wilhemina Von Sydow's Finishing School for Ladies. She laughed to herself. If those snobby rich parents knew what their sophisticated, debutante daughters were doing at school, they would question what type of finishing school Madame Von Sydow was running. Josie threw her head back, swirling long raven-black hair off her face. Her ponytail reached the middle of her back. She disliked knotting it in a tight bun or tying it up for formal occasions. The formal event at the fort was the officers' ball. Josie dreaded that stuffed-shirt affair. Her other escape was square dancing. She loved to dance and kick up her heels.

Her face, broad and high-cheeked, framed her deep-set eyes. An impish upturned nose and a wide, slightly seductive mouth added mischief to the smile that usually traced her lips. Her lithe body was visible though disguised underneath a high-necked bodice and petticoated frock. She received many admiring glances and slyly flaunted her body, much to her father's consternation.

She had witnessed this scene in the colonel's office before. Her father was a drunk. She hated his drinking, but with tender love would take him home and put him to bed. Her heartbreak was as genuine as her loathing to see him this way. "Daddy," she called softly, "it's me, Josie. Let's go home now." Her words startled the colonel out of his stupor.

"Oh, my love," he replied with a sigh. "Come here and help me. I'm so low-spirited."

Josie's sweet voice and touch soothed him. Soon she had him on his feet and headed for the cottage. "You know you shouldn't do this to yourself," she calmly chided him. "Why do you? Tell me."

"You wouldn't understand. It's between soldiers, and that, young woman, is something you know nothing about. They don't teach those things at your fancy ladies' school."

Josie had been at Fort Manning for five months. She had come on leave from school to nurse her ailing mother. Mrs. Julia Prentice had died three months after Josie arrived, and Josie stayed on to look after her father. She enjoyed her freedom from school. Josie had rebelled against Madame Von Sydow's frilly school from day one, but that was all in the past. At Fort Manning her high-spirited nature was unreined.

As Josie helped her stumbling father to the cottage, she pried deeper, trying to get to the root of her father's drinking. Her father slammed the door on further conversation. She could not budge him. Josie had overheard murmured conversations and gleaned information from blurted statements. She had a notion what was behind it, but the pieces of the puzzle were just that, pieces. The frustrating problem was, she had no one to talk with concerning her suspicions. She was at a loss to stop her father from drinking.

The sutler's store at Fort Manning was tucked away on the far side of the drill field, behind the stables. Shag Nickelson, an affable old-timer, ran the store. He had been a trapper, fur trader, and Army scout. In retirement Shag found his niche here. The U.S. Army did not officially condone sutlers, yet the stores played an important part in making military life more bearable. Items such as canned fruit, coffee, sugar, tea, and blankets were available. The most sought-after necessities, whiskey and tobacco, were usually in short supply. Shag's credit was easy. Too easy. Several of the soldiers took advantage of Shag's carefree manner and lagged behind in their payments. In his younger days Shag would have kicked ass and taken names on the men who owed him money. Now he relied on outside help.

Breed befriended the old-timer and had hammered out a collection arrangement on debts owed. Breed talked with the debtors; payment schedules were set up. Occasionally Breed resorted to intimidation. In return Shag gave him discounts on any purchases. This was a mutually satisfactory relationship for both men. Breed was shopping for .45 shells when Shag approached him. "Breed, I have . . . never mind." Shag paused, then turned to leave.

"You're draggin' your feet, my friend. What's on your mind?"

"I don't know how to put this."

"Tell me straight out." Breed laughed. "I'm a big boy." A quick smile creased his face.

"I'm having trouble collecting from one of your fellow sergeants. Actually there are two people."

"I need names, Shag. Then I'll have a chat with 'em."

"Bring your lunch," Shag warned him. "It will take that long. It's Fitz and his sawed-off sidekick, Corporal Calhoun. Fitz owes me four months of bills. Mostly whiskey," Shag threw in the tidbit of information. "Whenever I mention it he threatens to break my arm or he sends that half-wit corporal to spook me. Fitz is smart. He won't get his hands dirty."

Breed sat, listened, and said not a word. He stroked his chin as he thought how to best deal with this situation.

"Another thing. I've noticed the card games nearly always go in Fitz's favor. I think he and Calhoun are cheating but I can't prove it." Shag was not a whiner but he felt he had a legitimate complaint. "I don't know if he's cold deckin' the other players but there's a pattern. Several of the men have mentioned it. Again, no proof."

"Let me dwell on it. We'll see if we can't even up those debts and improve on the odds for our card players."

Payday at Fort Manning was three weeks late. A handful of soldiers were in the frame of mind to spend their money on cheap booze and card games. These card games were strictly against military regulations but took place anyway. The loading dock behind Shag's store was an ideal location. It was tucked out of sight and seldom if ever did an officer venture past. Late in the afternoon Sergeant Fitz, Corporal Calhoun, and three other soldiers showed up. They bought a bottle of rotgut and adjourned to the "card parlor." Breed and Shag watched a half-dozen games from the storeroom window. Fitz and Calhoun were winners. To catch them cheating would be damned hard to prove. "Shag, you're a cardsharp," Breed ribbed him. "No offense intended. Do you think Fitz can be beat?"

"That four-flusher," Shag replied with scorn. "Be like poppin' off a tom turkey comin' in after sweet corn. I'd like to play him clean poker. An hour and I'll tell you if he's worth a plug of chew." A sparkle was back in his eye. The thought of playing Fitz had Shag primed for action. "Hell, Breed. I'll even supply the rotgut. Free."

Several hours later the game folded. Fitz was boisterous. He bragged on his winnings and invited the losers to return tomorrow afternoon for a chance to redeem themselves. Shag and Breed talked at length about the game, players, and strategy. It grated on them to watch their friends fleeced by Fitz and Calhoun.

The following afternoon poker chips flew, dollars died, and whiskey was drunk with sheer intent. Shag left the front of the store and came back onto the dock. Fitz was winning and Calhoun was his usual somber self. The other players were down in the mouth, their pockets lighter. "Care if I sit in, Fitz?" Shag asked.

"Hell no," he replied in anticipation of bigger earnings. "If the store maid wants to lose money, I'll gladly oblige. Sit."

Shag tried to sit directly across from Fitz but Corporal Calhoun would not move. The sutler wanted to force Calhoun to change seats. Fitz and Calhoun always took the same places and sat directly across from each other. Shag was forced to sit beside one of the soldiers. Breed watched the game through the storeroom window. Shag's debut into the card game was an unmitigated calamity.

Breed watched the fiasco for as long as he could tolerate. He walked out the front door frustrated and in dire need of fresh air. He strolled aimlessly past the stalls and hay-filled lofts of the stable. As he passed under the loft that covered Shag's loading dock, he was dusted with straw chaff. Glancing up, Breed saw the heel of a boot protruding over the edge. He tiptoed to the ladder and painstakingly climbed it, not making a sound. When slightly above the prone figure, Breed saw the man was engrossed in the task at hand. The reason for Fitz's Irish luck at cards was lying belly down on the floor flashing signals to Corporal Calhoun.

Breed unholstered his pistol and jammed the barrel between the soldier's legs. The man twisted in pain and quickly got to his knees. Breed motioned to be quiet, then bade him to follow down the ladder. Breed covered the soldier as he stepped off the ladder. When

Breed recognized Private Honeywell he holstered his pistol. A painful grimace and fear etched the young soldier's face. "Honeywell, have you taken leave of your senses? What in the hell were you doing there?" The lad did not answer. "I'm takin' a guess Sergeant Fitz put you up to this." Again no reply from the soldier. "Don't go playing dumb on me, boy. What's he got on you?"

"He's blackmailing me," Honeywell reluctantly answered, but said no more.

"Why?" Breed demanded as Honeywell clammed up. "Lad, I have enough right now to hang your dumb ass."

"I borrowed a horse awhile back. Fitz found out and threatened to report me. You saw the rest."

Breed sought to reassure the young soldier. "Don't you worry about Fitz anymore. I'll take care of him." Breed grabbed the youth by the scruff of the neck and gently pushed him on his way. "You owe me one, Honeywell. And, lad, I'll give you a sound piece of advice. If I see you here again, you will be in front of the old man pronto."

"Thanks, Sarge. I'll do as you say." Honeywell was relieved and walked away with a slight limp.

Breed called to him. "Tell Fitz you got a case of the runs and had to leave," Breed warned. "Don't breathe a word of this to anyone." With the elimination of Fitz's cheating scam, Breed hustled to Shag's store and waited for their plan to unfold.

Shag intentionally drained the whiskey bottle,

knowing Fitz liked to drink while he played cards. Shag would wait him out.

"More whiskey, Shag," Fitz ordered. "It makes me play better."

The sutler made motions to stand, then slumped in his chair. "Give an old man a break," he complained. "Corporal Calhoun, would you hop up and get a new bottle. Hell, bring two. I'm plumb tuckered out."

The corporal was hesitant to leave the table. He looked at Fitz for approval and received a mere idea of a nod. Fitz, brimming with confidence, needled the corporal. "Hustle in there, boy, and get the booze. We'll wait for your return," Fitz chided his cohort.

Corporal Calhoun abruptly skidded his chair away from the table and stormed toward the door. Calhoun was in a huff over being called a boy in front of the other soldiers. He split the winnings with Fitz, which made him an equal partner, not a flunky. His anger deepened. Breed waited patiently inside the storeroom, hidden behind the tiered shelves. He swung a sock filled with sand in his hand. As the corporal strode past the pile of stacked blankets, Breed laid him out colder than a block of ice. Calhoun greeted the floor with a solid thud. Before Breed stepped back into the shadows he poured some whiskey over the prostrate figure. He then settled onto a comfortable seat of feed sacks. The rest was up to Shag.

After waiting anxiously for Calhoun's return, Fitz turned on Shag. "Where in the hell is your whiskey, Shag? That boy could have made some by now."

"Don't know, Sarge." Shag shrugged his bony shoulders. "He should have been back by now. Maybe he's drinking it all. Harder, why don't you go see if you can find him."

Private Harder disappeared into the store. He returned shortly with two bottles. "Damned fool's passed out." Harder gleefully spread the word. "He's stiff as a board in the back room." The private nodded with his head in the direction of the storeroom.

"Calhoun's what?" Fitz asked. He didn't trust Harder.

"Out cold. I kicked him but he didn't move. Smells like a brewery," Private Harder answered with a wide grin on his face.

Sergeant Fitz felt his stomach turn. He'd lost a helper but still had an ace upstairs. It would make the game more difficult but he would manage. With a casual glance to the loft, Fitz realized the holes were unattended. A sinking feeling gripped him. Not to worry, he thought with shaky confidence. I can use the reflection off the window as a backup. Fitz looked at the window. It was closed. He was flummoxed. All of his cheating schemes were negated. He would have to play with skill to win. "Let me deal 'em, Shag," Fitz asked forcefully. "My Irish luck's still good."

"My pleasure, Shamus. You will need some of that luck. The drinks are on me, lads."

The first two hands went to "Poker Face" Shag, who bluffed Fitz down twice. Harder won the next two. Fitz, until now cutting a fat hog, was at wits' end. His upstairs player never showed a sign, his coworker was passed out, and the window was closed. A cheater's instinct told him to get out, but that might arouse suspicions. The look of despair on Fitz's face was worth all the moneys owed.

Two hours later Sergeant Fitz threw his cards down in disgust. "I've had it. I'm broke and owe you part of my next two paychecks, Shag." Fitz threatened playfully, "No more."

Shag had controlled the game through slick dealing and lots of bluff. Fitz had consumed the better part of a bottle of whiskey, which did not help his game. Shag watched happily as the other players recouped their losses. "I thank you, gentlemen." The sutler smiled at the players as he raked in the winnings from the last hand. "Sergeant Fitz, I'll square your account with these earnings, if that's all right with you?"

Fitz gave him a weak smile which barely disguised an inner fury ready to erupt. "Oh, Sergeant Fitz," Shag asked with mock concern. "Please take Corporal Calhoun with you on the way out."

The card game over, the players left with their earnings. However, the real winnings had been to watch the sarge get shellacked. Fitz barged into the storeroom and nearly tripped over Corporal Calhoun. He reached under the corporal's armpits and yanked him upright. Even drunk Fitz was a bear. He carried Calhoun out of the store. The sergeant was in high dudgeon, not for the monetary loss but at being made a fool of in front of the other soldiers. Fitz carried Calhoun to the water trough and unceremoniously dumped him in. Damn that stupid fool. His drunken stupor was plain dumb. Calhoun floated for a few seconds before he slowly sank beneath the surface. Several long moments passed before he exploded out of the water, coughing and sputtering. The corporal stood upright in the trough, momentarily blinded as water ran down his face.

"You cheap drunk, passing out on me like that," Fitz chewed him out. "It will cost you. Half of my losses for the evening." Fitz, nearly shouting, poked him in the chest. "And, boy, I mean to tell you. We lost!"

"Ah, Sarge," Calhoun whined. "I must have tripped. I'm tellin' you I wasn't drunk. Really."

"The hell you say. I pulled you to your feet two hours later and you were out cold. What the hell you call that, catnapping?" Fitz continued to berate him. "You smelled like a damned saloon."

"Don't push me too goddanged far, Fitz. If word gets out tha—"

Fitz slapped him hard across the face. A red welt began to appear. "You little shit," he seethed. "I've made you what you are. Don't pull no double cross on me. You're way out of your class." Fitz confronted Calhoun and stood an inch from his face. "Don't you forget it, boy!"

"We'll see about that. Don't you go leanin' too hard on me," Calhoun snapped as Fitz turned his back and walked away.

Sergeant Fitz left Calhoun and headed for his quarters. His mind raced, trying to figure out what went wrong. Where in the hell was Honeywell? Did Shag suspect anything? Fitz's gut feeling was that he had been set up.

Shag and Breed heard the ruckus in front of the store. They waited in the storeroom until all was quiet. Breed was comfortably reclined on the feed sacks, sock in hand. A wide grin creased his face.

"Nice work, lad. I don't know what you did but it sure worked." Shag gleefully rubbed his hands together. "I truly enjoyed those games. Was Calhoun any trouble?"

"Nope," drawled Breed. "He sure is thick-skulled. I had to hit him twice. Other than a sore head he'll be fine tomorrow." Breed laughed, then added, "That's if he lives until then."

"What was those boys doin' to rig them games?"

"Sergeant Fitz had extra help. He was blackmailing Private Honeywell. The private read the players' hands from the loft then flashed signals down to Calhoun. The corporal somehow passed that information on to Fitz and he would play or bet accordingly." Breed got to his feet and walked toward the window. "I noticed yesterday Fitz kept glancing at this window. After he left I sat in his chair. The window reflects part of the table and would reveal the hands of players seated beneath it."

"That's why those two always sit in the same places. Calhoun wouldn't let me squeeze in yesterday. Made me sit beside Private Harder." Shag was pleased they had busted up the crooked card games. "I can't thank you enough, Breed, for helping me. I'll fetch a bottle of some good whiskey. Let's have a drink."

CHAPTER
7

The arrival of fifteen soldiers at Fort Manning fired up the rumor mill. One rumor was the men were replacements. Several of the younger soldiers in the fort believed their enlistments were over, tours of duty at Fort Manning finished. The old-timers sat back and watched the spectacle. This had happened too many times before. The veterans reserved judgment. If indeed the fifteen were replacements, there would be ample cause for celebration. If not, the routine would continue as usual.

Breed and Stills were out of the blistering sun, repairing gear in the stable. The saddles, bridles, and panniers continually needed work. They watched as five of the soldiers went directly to Colonel Prentice's office. The remaining men brought the extra horses to the stable. The livery private took the horses as the corporal from the detail stopped in front of Breed. He was young, of medium build, and rough-cut. Despite his weanling appearance, a closer look revealed a hardened soldier well schooled in the art of desert and Indian warfare.

"Afternoon, Sergeant." He nodded. "I'm Corporal Fisher. Could you assist us?" he asked politely. "We will stay the night and return to Fort Prescott tomorrow. Could you secure quarters for us? And possibly something to eat. It's been a long day."

"No problem, Corporal Fisher," Breed offered. "We were hoping for new blood, but not this time, huh? Off tomorrow?"

"Yep. We escorted those five pettifoggers. Believe me"—he shook his head in wonderment—"they needed all the help we could give them. I understand the Indians are uprisin' all over this country. We have been ordered to return to Fort Prescott as soon as possible."

Breed was smiling. "Lad, where did you learn 'pettifoggers'? I haven't heard the word in years."

"My father had a loathing for anyone vaguely connected with the legal profession. That was how he addressed those 'professionals.' " The young man chuckled. "Damned if he didn't turn out to be a circuit judge."

"Dave, help these boys with their horses." Breed threw his gloves at Stills. "I'll be back shortly. Let's go, Corporal."

The next morning Corporal Fisher and his men headed out. Fort Manning buzzed with speculation over the presence of the five remaining officers. These men were sequestered in Colonel Prentice's office and only appeared for a midmorning break. The midday meal was served in Colonel Prentice's office. When outside of the colonel's office, the five men stayed to themselves.

Breed took the noon meal in his quarters. He ate without gusto, simply refueling. The heat tempered his appetite. As he returned to work, he walked past the chow hall, and overheard the gossip. "They are here to check on the colonel. They're on to his drinking," volunteered a soldier.

"Nope, you're wrong. The payroll has been short," someone cut in. "They have figured out Fitz and his card games." They all laughed.

"Enough of this crap." The gruff voice of Sergeant Fitz interrupted the conversation. "You sound like a bunch of old ladies. Move your butts. We have work to do."

"Ah, come on, Sarge," pleaded a soldier. "What's goin' on? Tell us."

"It's a court-martial," he replied. "That's all I know. Now move."

Breed searched his mind but could find nothing that warranted a court-martial at Fort Manning. Maybe Fitz and Calhoun were still mad. He laughed at the thought. Breed spent the next hours in the stable working by himself, and more than once cursed Stills for not showing. When Dave arrived late in the afternoon, he was sullen. Breed prodded him. "You're damned serious, Dave. What's wrong?"

Stills sat mute for a spell, disinclined to talk. He absentmindedly tugged at his mustache, then measured his words. "Breed, you have any idea who them boys are? Or why they're here?"

"Nope, and can't say I give a damn either. I've done

nothing to get those legal vultures onto me."

"My friend," Still snapped, "you *are* the reason they're here." Stills let his words sink in. He said nothing else.

"Talk, man," Breed implored. "Come on, Dave. I'd like to think I'm big enough to handle it."

Dave hesitated, then spoke his mind. "I was requested to report to Colonel Prentice's office. Those officers are holding court-martial proceedings with murder charges pending. You are standing at the head of the line."

"Murder." Breed whispered. "Whose may I ask?"

"Will Williams," was Dave's tight reply.

Breed was dumbfounded. A prickly feeling traced its way along the hairline on his neck. His stomach knotted and his palms turned sweaty. The flashback to Twin Buttes was vivid. He could see Williams's chest partially covered by the front bead. The rifle recoiled upward in slow motion. Through the smoke Breed knew he had hit Will.

Breed sat slowly on a hay bale. "Williams." He choked on his name. Stills merely nodded. "Let me guess who pressed charges."

"Of course," Dave answered. "The man never misses an opportunity."

"Fitz must be enjoying this immensely."

"One of those law dudes will be lookin' you up shortly. Wants to find the *facts,*" Dave told him with a wide grin.

"You were in there with them?" Stills bodded his

head. "What did you tell them?" Breed pressed his friend.

Dave paused and let Breed dangle a little.

"Tell me, Dave. What did you say?" Urgency laced his voice.

"The truth." Dave smiled for the first since his return to the stable. "I told them I didn't see a thing. I explained about my wound and how I was taking care of it."

"They believed you?"

"Who knows. I do know one thing. There are some mighty poor-minded officers in there with Colonel Prentice. I guess that's to be expected. Ever heard of Colonel Bull Butkus?" Breed frowned his reply. "He's the convening officer. Got his name at the Battle of Bull Run. A real hard-ass."

"They sound tough." Breed searched for some reassurance from Stills. He got none.

"Between you and me? I think they have their minds made up. The only one who seems open-minded is Captain Morris. He's wet behind the ears but tries to be fair. My horse-tradin' sense tells me the bigger brass are decided."

"Thanks, my friend. I can't say I needed this. I do appreciate your help."

Breed picked at the evening meal and left it for a walk and some fresh air. As he walked on the huge drill field he was approached from behind by a young, "freshly minted" officer. "Excuse me, Sergeant Stalwart. May I have a word with you?"

"Yes, sir." He saluted. "Do you mind if we walk?"

"No, that's fine. I'm Captain Morris, your legal officer. I've been appointed by the convening officer to handle your case."

Breed shrugged off the legal jargon. "From what I've heard the verdict is already in."

The captain flushed, then bristled. "Sergeant, I'll make two things absolutely clear. I'm my own man and no one pushes me around. Also, I give any man the benefit of the doubt until proven dead wrong." The young officer spoke forcefully. "If you want to piss this whole thing off and give up, say the word and I'm gone."

"Relax, Captain Morris." Breed sought to calm him. "It sounds better already. Where do we go from here?"

"I've gone through your record and it's excellent. Why not start by telling me exactly what happened on the Twin Buttes patrol."

Breed talked himself hoarse. He patiently explained in detail the sequence of events. He withheld no information as he relived the devastating day at Twin Buttes. Captain Morris waited until Breed had finished. "You admit you shot Williams?"

"Captain Morris, are we talking the same language?" Breed asked in frustration. "I told you exactly what happened. What's the problem?"

"You openly confess to killing a fellow soldier. That is going to be difficult to deal with."

"It was in the line of duty," Breed replied.

"There's your problem. It's murder," the captain replied coolly.

"Says you," Breed lashed out, his anger rising.

"No, not me. Says the American Articles of War. I'll quote you the paragraph if you like. You just can't go around shooting other soldiers."

An awkward silence fell between the men as they wandered around the drill field. Breed broke the silence. "Tell me something, sir. Have you ever seen action?"

"Yes, I have," was the testy response from the officer.

"May I ask where, sir?"

"I was the communications officer with General Grant. At Shiloh," he stated with pride.

"Did you ever pull a trigger? Watch the man you just shot die?" No response from the officer. "Did you? Damn it, sir," Breed pleaded. "We're not talking about the annual officers' turkey shoot. We're talking about killing men. Men like you. Like Williams." Breed felt he was making progress with the officer. His temper simmered as he faced the officer. "Have you fought the Indians, sir? Do you have an insight how they think? Or what makes them fight and hate the white man?"

"Does it really matter? Is it pertinent to this case?"

"You bet it is." Breed pressed his point. "If you don't understand the Indian and what makes him tick, then we'll not understand each other. Plain and simple." Breed had nothing more to say to the officer. Breed didn't like his brief glimpse at this career officer's outlook.

"I have a request, Sergeant Stalwart. Can you write?" The officer was embarrassed after he asked the question. "I apologize. I had to ask."

"I understand. Yes, I can write. Why?"

"Excellent. Write your report of the Twin Buttes patrol just as you told me. Give me the report when you're finished."

"Sir, Colonel Prentice already has it."

"Ah, he does? Good. I'll get it from him."

"Will it do any good to go over my report?" Breed wanted to know.

"Yes, you'd be surprised. You have given me several ideas which might help. I apologize for my lack of military field experience, and appreciate your straightforward manner." The officer offered his hand to Breed. "You'll be called in front of the board tomorrow afternoon for an informal hearing. Thanks again. Good night."

The following afternoon Breed reported to Colonel Prentice's office. The five-man court-martial board was seated awaiting his arrival. The room was sweltering hot, which added to the discomfort of the men present. After being briefed by the convening officer, Colonel Bull Butkus, Breed recounted his version of the ill-fated patrol. His powers of recall were nearly pictographic. He spared no details. The board methodically cross-examined him. They grilled hard and probed deep. Breed felt these men didn't understand the circumstances or the situation. They were academy-taught, with textbook ideas and war-college training. He laughed inwardly and thought, There is the right way, the wrong way, and the Army way. How can I get them to relate to my point of view?

"These informal proceedings will adjourn and reconvene at 1800 hours," Colonel Butkus stated.

"Sir," Captain Morris addressed the colonel. "According to paragraph 51-B subarticle 2A in the Articles of War, any informal hearing is required to seat one third of the board consisting of enlisted personnel. Subarticle 3A states this also applies to formal inquiries. I believe this will allow for one enlisted man to be included on the board for future hearings."

"One moment, Captain Morris." Colonel Butkus huddled with the other board members. One of the officers thumbed through a thick leatherbound volume. They referred to the appropriate articles and agreed on their findings. "I stand corrected, Captain. Will you see to this matter?" Colonel Butkus addressed Breed. "Sergeant Stalwart, we won't require your presence this evening. We are adjourned, gentlemen. Dismissed."

Breed was depressed; a foreboding feeling of doom engulfed him. Stills's words were fresh in his mind. "They seem to have their minds made up." Breed's sentiments exactly. Those men simply did not know or understand the Indians. Breed walked as if it would lessen his burden. His aimless wanderings brought him by officers' row. Realizing he was nearly on sacred ground he turned quickly and headed for the stables. The sight of a woman walking toward him cleared his head. As the woman drew closer, Breed recognized Josie Prentice. She walked directly to him with a smooth gait. Her green eyes met his and she smiled. Breed tipped his hat. "Evening, Miss Prentice."

"Such formality." She laughed. "Evening, Sergeant Stalwart. Please, call me Josie. Miss Prentice sounds so stuffy, like that awful girls' school." She reached out and touched his arm. "You've been in with those officers, haven't you?" Breed nodded numbly. "I can tell. After a visit with them everyone looks ruffled. Rest out here, they can't hear us."

Breed was slightly uncomfortable with this raven-haired beauty. She was unsettling with her straight talk and open manner.

"I'm sorry the court-martial is going the way it is," Josie commented. Breed jerked his head around to meet her eyes. "Oh, I didn't mean it to sound like that." She dropped off talking. Breed's look made her painfully aware she had already said too much.

Breed shrugged. "It's all right. I have the same feeling. You just made it official, that's all."

"Breed . . . I mean Sergeant Stalwart. I'm terribly sorry. Oh, hell. I don't know what I mean." She grabbed his arm and gave him an affectionate squeeze. Then she burst into tears. Moments later she spoke. "Look at me. Shooting off my big mouth, then crying like a baby." She searched through her hand purse, then her pockets, for a hankie. "I don't suppose you have a handkerchief?"

Breed shook his head. "All I can offer is a wet bandanna." He laughed as he caught her smile.

"Well, let me have it. Thanks."

Breed untied the bandanna from his neck and gave it to her. She dabbed at her eyes and wiped the tears from

129

her cheeks. She handed it back and spoke dejectedly. "Aren't you going to ask me how I know?" She dangled the question.

"How do you know?" Breed replied immediately.

"Papa said the board has scant choice. They have to find you guilty or every soldier in the U.S. Army will be shooting whomever he wants. He also said the witness reports were cold, hard facts."

"He would be referring to Sergeant Fitz, wouldn't he?"

"That's odd you should mention him. You are correct," she added. "What do you know about Sergeant Fitz?"

"Not much. I don't like the man, and stay away from him whenever possible. I'll tell you one thing—" Breed cautioned her, "He's a man without scruples."

"I realize this will sound strange, but he appears to have some hold over Papa. My father seems to be afraid of the man."

"Why do you say that?" Breed was curious about her statement.

"Last week Papa met with Sergeant Fitz. The day you all returned from Twin Buttes. They got skunk drunk. As I helped Papa to the cottage, he mumbled something about being forced into a hopeless situation. He clammed up, then began to ramble on about Fredericksburg."

"I told you, I don't like Fitz, but I doubt he's dumb enough to buck an officer."

"Breed," Josie challenged him. "You're dead wrong.

He has something on my father. Is there any way you could check on him? Please." She clutched his arm, and was squeezing it hard without being aware of it.

Breed realized Josie was desperate. He knew he would need more information than she had given him. "I have a friend in personnel. He owes me a favor. Let me see what he can come up with."

"Thank you, Breed. There is something terribly evil between those two," Josie added. "Whatever it is, it drives Papa to the depths of depression and makes him drink himself dead drunk."

Breed offered his arm to Josie, then patted her hand reassuringly. "Don't you fret. I'll find something. May I escort you to your cottage?"

"I would be delighted." She smiled. "Lead on, escort."

There was no action from the court-martial board. The waiting wore thin on Breed, a man of prompt action. The hours dragged along painfully slow. To occupy time Breed paid a visit to the personnel clerk and collected on the favor. The revelations were informative but inconclusive. Colonel Prentice and Sergeant Fitz had served in the same area of operations at Fredericksburg during the Civil War. Each had been transferred four times. More interesting was the fact they had the identical transfer assignments. If there was a connection, it was not obvious from the records. Breed passed this information on to Josie although it appeared to be of little value.

At morning muster and quarters, the officer of the

day, Captain Cummings, added this final order to the plan of the day. "Performance evaluations and promotion recommendations will be turned in to me by 1500 hours today. Questions?"

Breed thought this strange. They were not due for another week. "Sir, why the hurry. We have another week."

"Orders from above, Sergeant Stalwart. Besides, it should be fairly clear by now who is up for promotion or advancement. Get them in today, gentlemen. Dismissed."

Captain Cummings corraled Breed before he went to work. They were alone. "Breed, I don't understand this stampede for evaluations either. I'll say one thing for certain: You can't be recommended or evaluated because of this current court-martial fiasco. Between us, this hurry-up job and the judical proceedings are aimed directly at you."

"Thanks, Captain Cummings. I appreciate your truthfulness." Breed spoke his mind. "It chafes my ass to be at the mercy of those legal hatchet men. It isn't right."

"Right? What in the hell does that have to do with it?" Breed thought he had overstepped himself. The officer continued. "You want to know what galls me even more? They will promote some 'good ole boy' and I'll have to carry his dumb ass until either I retire or the Indians mercifully kill him." The officer was mad. "I had already put you in for first sergeant. *Right!*" he scoffed. "It's chickenshit. That's what it is."

• • •

"Gentlemen," stated Colonel Bull Butkus, "on this date, September twelfth, 1880, Military Division of the Pacific, Department of Arizona, Divisional Headquarters Prescott . . ." The colonel paused and took in a deep breath. "These formal court-martial proceedings will commence in the United States Army fort, Fort Manning, at 1300 hours. This case involves the United States Army's Judge Advocate and the Judical Review Board versus Sergeant James Stalwart. These hearings are under the jurisdiction of Convening Officer Colonel Hiram Butkus. For the record I will introduce each member of the board by rank and duty.

"Colonel Butkus, convening officer. Major Hunter, judge advocate. Captain Pendleton, legal officer. Captain Kuster, legal officer. Captain Morris, legal officer for the accused. First Sergeant Alcorn, enlisted personnel representative."

Colonel Bull Butkus scanned the table and spotted Major Hunter. "Major Hunter, since this is a formal proceeding, would you please swear in Sergeant Stalwart."

The major, his face disfigured from a Civil War minié ball, faced Breed. His right eye was cocked at an awkward angle, the side of his face shiny scar tissue. The major stated the legal requirements Breed was obligated to honor. Breed repeated the oath. A nod from the major set the proceeding in motion.

"Gentlemen, be seated," Colonel Butkus offered. "Major Hunter will conduct the proceeding from this point forward. Major."

Major Hunter's voice reflected the gravity of the proceedings. "Thank you, Colonel Butkus. This board has received testimony from expert witness. The board has attempted to remain impartial while weighing the evidence. As presiding officer, I ask for final comments or introduction of new testimony before we render a verdict." The major looked at each member of the board, his face angled awkwardly to compensate for his wound. No one came forward except Captain Morris.

"Sir, I request permission to proceed on a new line of testimony. Please bear with me. The following questions will serve a point."

"Very well, proceed," replied the major as he sat.

"I would like to ask each member of the board if he fought in the Great War and if so, where?" Captain Morris turned to Colonel Bull Butkus.

"Yes. Bull Run, and I also served under Major General George B. McClellan at Antietam."

"Yes," Major Hunter replied. "I fought with Major General Hancock, at Cemetery Hill."

"Affirmative. Chancellorsville, then Gettysburg," was Captain Pendleton's professional, hard-core answer.

"I fought at Chickamauga. There I was wounded." Captain Kuster dipped his shoulder. His empty right sleeve was pinned back.

"I proudly marched with the best damned general in the war, General William Tecumseh Sherman," stated the outspoken First Sergeant Alcorn.

"I put in my duty with General Grant, at Shiloh,"

Captain Morris added with a trace of pride. "Gentlemen, is it not a fair statement to say a soldier captured by either side during that honorable war would have been humanely treated? His status as a prisoner guaranteed."

To a man the board members agreed. "Sir," Captain Morris petitioned Major Hunter. "One final question."

"Carry on, Captain. But I must ask to where these questions are leading." The major subconsciously rubbed his scarred face.

"Sir, I am seeking to define a subtle point in the proceedings."

"Very well. Proceed."

"Have any of the board members fought in any Indian campaigns?" Major Hunter and First Sergeant Alcorn were the only members to respond in the affirmative. Major Hunter had fought with Major George Forsythe at Beecher's Island, and Alcorn with Captain Tenedor Ten Eych.

"We were the relief column from Fort Phil Kearny," Alcorn explained as he spoke without permission.

Captain Morris tried to smooth over the breech in procedure. "For those of you who don't know, Captain Ten Eych was to reinforce Captain Fetterman and his eighty men. By the time Ten Eych arrived, all eighty-one soldiers had been massacred."

"Captain Morris, your point?" asked Major Hunter, his eyes not focusing on the captain.

"Sir, we are talking inconsistent judicial systems. We can not judge a man's actions today while using antiquated Civil War standards. Two divergent styles of warfare shouldn't be made equal in the eyes of the law."

"Explain the meaning of your last statement, Captain," Colonel Bull Butkus asked.

"Sir, in Indian warfare we are faced with an enemy who knows no law and respects no white man. He has refined the art of murder, torture, and mutilation. While we judge Sergeant Stalwart, we must consider the circumstances under which he acted the way he did."

"Nevertheless we must look at the facts. Need I remind you, Captain?" Colonel Butkus reprimanded the officer.

"I agree, sir, but we must ask why he apparently acted inconsistently with military standards of acceptable conduct."

"May I talk, sir?" First Sergeant Alcorn interrupted again in complete disregard for procedure. Major Hunter looked at Captain Morris and got a nod of approval. "I believe Captain Morris is makin' a point that's valid and must be looked at careful. Forgive my bluntness, but has any of you ever seen a man's head exploded over a small roastin' fire? Or seen his guts pulled slowly out through a hole in his stomach?" Alcorn looked at each member of the board eyeball to eyeball. "Have you ever seen what's left of a soldier what's been skinned alive?" Major Hunter met and held Alcorn's glare. "We ain't talkin' field casualties here. We're talking cold-blooded murder and torture. Killin' to intimidate and frighten. Murder for pleasure.

If we are to judge Sergeant Stalwart, we must consider them circumstances." Alcorn sat.

An awkward silence stilled the room. Major Hunter cleared his throat. "Colonel Butkus, may I speak off the record?" The officer agreed. "Members of the board. We are faced with a most difficult judgment. We have heard of Captain Fetterman's costly and fatal blunder. I believe First Sergeant Alcorn could elaborate upon the two full days he spent picking up the remains of his comrades." Alcorn dipped his head slightly in accord. "I won't burden you with the nearly-fifty-percent casualty rate at Beecher's Island. What needs to be stressed and understood is that in an Indian campaign, we are dealing with an unwritten code of lawlessness, violence, and brutality." The major's face was flushed, the scars chalky white. "We cannot ignore the Articles of War, but we must be cognizant of the field of battle. In this snakebitten Department of Arizona the Indians give no quarter and expect none in return. I am relieved to know there are men like Sergeant Stalwart in the service." The major looked at Breed. "I'd gladly have him in my command and go into battle beside him. Capture out here is not worse than death, it *is* death."

The major sat, relieved he had defended Breed in a manner the board would appreciate and understand.

"This is preposterous," thundered the professional soldier, Captain Pendleton. He violently slammed both hands on the tabletop, stood quickly, and knocked his chair over. The board members were rudely jarred out of their reflections of Major Hunter's well-chosen words. "We are talking about the deliberate shooting of a United States Army soldier by another United States soldier." The captain stood ramrod straight. "It isn't a question of whether or not we agree with the accused's actions. Neither is the theater or the command under which he served. The crux of the matter is, we cannot have soldiers shooting other soldiers." The officer was firm and uncompromising. "The facts support the law. Sergeant Stalwart is guilty and we must set the precedent to preserve the very survival of military justice in the U.S. Army."

First Sergeant Alcorn leapt to his feet, shaking his fist at the officer. "I pray to God I never have to serve under you in an Indian fight. *Sir!*" Alcorn hurled the insult at the polished officer.

"Why, how dare—" Captain Pendleton challenged.

"Enough," shouted Colonel Bull Butkus. "These court-martial proceedings will recess until 0900 tomorrow morning. Dismissed."

"Sergeant Stalwart," Major Hunter addressed him. "Will you please stand to receive the recommendations of the court-martial board."

Breed stood on reflex. His guts churned with a bitter feeling he had failed. He also felt Captain Morris and Major Hunter had failed to change any of the board's opinions.

"On this day, the sixteenth of September, 1880, at 0900, it is the majority opinion of the court-martial board that Sergeant James Stalwart is guilty of murder of Trooper Will Williams. After a thorough and impartial investigation, and lengthy review, the board's four-to-two majority opinion is that the preponderance of evidence, the accused's own admission of guilt, are overwhelming. The board also felt this type of action must not be tolerated. A precedent-setting opinion must be rendered." The major continued to read the recommendations without glancing from the paper. "Therefore, within the thirty-day appeal period, Sergeant Stalwart will be confined to the stockade and will be relieved of all military rank and duties. If after thirty days the appeal process is denied by both the Military Jurisprudence Board and Appellate Judge Advocate, Sergeant James Stalwart will be executed at 0700 on the fifteenth day of October, 1880, by a military firing squad at Fort Manning." The major looked at Breed, a bitter look on his disfigured face. "So decrees this board. Signed Major Huntington Hunter, Presiding Officer, and Colonel Hiram Butkus, Convening Officer."

Breed couldn't accept this decision and spoke to Major Hunter. "Sir, may I address the board?"

"Concerning what?" Colonel Butkus rudely cut in.

"Sir, I don't feel the board—"

"Sergeant, be quiet," Colonel Bull Butkus snapped at Breed. "We read your report. Heard your testimony." The colonel counted off on his fingers. "You had adequate legal counsel. There is nothing more to be gained by further discussion."

"But, sir," Captain Morris interjected, "he has the right—"

"Rights be damned!" Colonel Butkus exploded. "I have bent over backwards to protect this man's rights. Who protected Will Williams's rights? We rendered our decision and will stand by it." The colonel turned to the guard detail posted by the door. "Captain Wainright, Sergeant at Arms, escort the prisoner to the stockade forthwith."

The officer, Sergeant Ellis, and two armed soldiers stepped forward, took Breed from Colonel Prentice's office, and led him to the stockade.

CHAPTER
8

Breed did not adjust to his confinement. He felt like a caged spirit, ate little, and slept fitfully. The loss of freedom made him desperate. He pleaded with First Sergeant Alcorn, Sergeant of the Guard, for time out of the stockade. First Sergeant Alcorn promised to do his best. The sergeant was sympathetic and felt Breed had been railroaded in his court-martial.

Alcorn was good on his word. The next day Breed was on work detail hauling water, splitting wood, and stable detail. He relished the opportunity to work again and attacked the tasks with a measured fury. Some men might have felt indignation working with the misfits and troublemakers on the details. Breed did not. Most of the young kids did not know better or were trying to beat the system. Breed enjoyed their company and got along well with them.

The detail sergeants knew Breed and worked well with him. They were respectful and knew he would not need supervision. To the contrary, the sergeants liked having Breed, because his work ethic rubbed off on the younger men. The details were trouble-free. Every fifth day Sergeant Fitz drew guard detail. Fitz deliberately made the day miserable for Breed. Fitz delighted in mustering his details at the hottest time of the day or ordering stable detail after midnight.

One of the field sergeants had been thrown from his horse and was laid up in the infirmary. Sergeant Fitz assumed his guard duty. This meant Fitz had two extra days to try and break Breed. The lurking possibility of a firing squad, plus the misunderstood motives behind the death of Will Williams, cracked Breed's composure. He let Sergeant Fitz get to him, something he had sworn not to let happen. Fitz was putting him through extra rifle drills in the hope of breaking his will. The rifle used, weighted and plugged, tipped the scales at twenty-eight pounds and was referred to affectionately as the attitude piece. "Aren't you getting tired of this game, Fitz?" Breed baited. "I'll be damned if I'll let you beat me."

Sergeant Fitz flushed angrily and stood within an inch of Breed's face. "You will address me as Sergeant Fitzpatrick when you speak," he shouted. To emphasize his point he jabbed a finger into Breed's chest.

"On your Blarney-stone head I will," Breed retorted. "How about 'Mick' or 'Mackerel-snapper'?"

Fitz's quick Irish temper flared. He violently grabbed

Breed's rifle. Breed chucked the rifle as Fitz pulled on it. The heavy barrel hit the sergeant on the forehead and opened a nasty, gushing cut. Fitz stood dazed, then pressed his hand to the wound. He stared at his blood-covered hand. Breed did the only reasonable thing. He hit Fitz with a stinging uppercut. The big Irishman was a seasoned brawler but Breed blindsided him. It was no contest. Fitz went down to the ground like a felled tree. Breed looked at the startled corporal on guard detail.

"Corporal, escort me to the stockade. Then return here and assist Sergeant Fitz." The confused soldier blankly nodded and obeyed.

The following morning the jingling of keys awakened Breed. Captain Butler, the officer of the day, flanked by two soldiers entered Breed's cell. "On your feet, Mister Stalwart." Breed slipped his weight off the cot and slowly stood. "Extend your hands to the front," ordered the captain. One of the soldiers circled behind Breed, slipped a chain around his waist, and locked it to the iron bracelets on his outstretched wrists. Breed could not raise his hands higher than mid-chest. "You will wear these shackles every time you go outside. Private, escort the prisoner to Colonel Prentice's office."

Colonel Prentice frowned deeply. The scowl high-lighted his bloodhound jowls and darkened his blood-shot eyes. "Mister Stalwart. I call you Mister because you have no rank," the colonel belittled Breed. "You have assaulted a noncommissioned officer. May I hear your explanation for this outrageous behavior?"

Sergeant Fitz stood behind and off to one side of the officer. A thick bandage and gauze wrap covered his forehead.

"Sir, I have no answer." He knew it would be futile to accuse Fitz of petty harassment he could not prove.

"Very well. You will be confined to the stockade for ten days. And receive one meal per diem. If there are further transgressions, you will be severely disciplined. Understood? Captain Smyth, return the prisoner to the stockade."

Time was dead. For Breed the days were a combination of frustration and boredom. He read, but the supply of books was limited. He whittled a new set of pistol grips for his .45. This presented a challenge because he didn't have the gun with him and the small pocketknife was inadequate. Stills stopped by and talked. "You seem to enjoy this good life," Dave kidded him.

"You bet. Up at 0900. Breakfast in my room. It's the best way to go." Breed tried to keep a straight face but failed.

"I've got some interesting news." Dave didn't rush into it but let Breed stew in anticipation. "Remember how quickly Walking Tall left us? I found out why. He joined with a bunch of Mexican renegades, Campesino included, and attacked General Clemments. With those stolen rifles they nearly wiped out our soldiers. Fort Gilpin was abandoned. The troopers made their successful stand at Mesita Flats."

"It should have been us, Dave, fighting down there."

Breed laughed bitterly. "I wouldn't be here now."

"Apparently the Mexicans felt Fort Gilpin threatened their access to Mexico and the Sierra Madres. The pressure's off now." Dave continued his explanation, "There isn't a fort in the entire southern approach to the desert basin. Walking Tall let us go as another example of what happens to whites who nose around Twin Buttes."

"I'll tell you one person who never wants to go near Twin Buttes," Breed offered.

"Me either. Once was enough. We won't be so lucky if there is a next time." Dave laughed. "I would imagine after Colonel Prentice tries to explain his way out of that fiasco, there won't be future military operations into the area."

"Dave, I'm not sure how much more of this I can stand."

"Stick with it," Dave encouraged.

"That's easy for you to say. You ever been locked up?"

"Nope." Stills shook his head. "As long as I stay clear of Fitz, I'll be safe. Remember those stolen rifles?" Dave glanced at Breed. "Other than the gunnery officer being demoted, nothing happened. No clues, no suspects, no nothin'. The army investigation team left with *nada*." Dave saved the best for last. "First Sergeant Alcorn mentioned a replacement shipment of rifles due shortly."

"When?" Breed perked up. "What did he tell you?"

"He wasn't volunteering much information. Soon

though. Colonel Prentice ordered a new armory built."

"Send Alcorn over if you see him. Tell him it's important." After Dave left, Breed began to plot his revenge against Fitz. Those new rifles would be too much of a temptation for Fitz to pass up. Alcorn would play a key role if Breed could talk him into going along with his idea.

It was early evening when the first sergeant dropped by. "Breed, there is something stickin' in my craw. I come to apologize about that farce . . ."

" 'Nuff said, Gunner. You don't owe me a thing. We both know it was a bad joke," Breed gently interrupted. "I want to thank you for your help. I hope it won't cost you." They had been in the army long enough to know bucking the brass could cost a man his promotions, orders, and duty stations.

"Not to worry, Breed." Alcorn calmed his fears. "I didn't get where I am by being a damned fool. I've made some friends over the years."

"Good. How would you like to set up Fitz. I mean really nail him."

"I'd love to. The man is a black mark on the military. Fill me in."

"I've got a sneaking suspicion Fitz was behind the rifle heist. I can't prove it but I feel it." Breed described the wagon incident, the ambush, and the loose window in the armory. Alcorn listened in disbelief.

"That's plumb stupid. Just like Fitz," Alcorn added. "Breed, that's a capital offense. A firing squad for sure."

"I know that, Gunner." Breed then forced a smile. "Be careful talking about firing squads. I'm a little touchy on the subject. Think of Fitz. His greed. He knows no rules. Hell, he makes his own." Breed continued to sweet-talk Alcorn. "What better way for Fitz to pocket lots of money?"

"Why, that back-shootin' bastard. We oughta turn him in."

"Slow down," Breed patiently explained. "Dave told me about the new shipment of rifles. Listen to my plan. If we succeed, Fitz will hang himself. I won't bullshit you. If it backfires, we're civilians pronto. You understand?"

Alcorn nodded grimly. For the next hour the two friends worked over details of the plan. "So we are agreed?" Breed questioned the first sergeant.

"We are," answered Alcorn. "It's a shame we won't see the results of our work. This is gonna take time to bear fruit. Fitz might be a civilian before it happens."

"That's true, Gunner. But once you double-cross an Indian, you've got an enemy for life. We'll let Fitz worry about it." They shook hands on the deal. Now to wait for the rifles and watch Fitz make his move.

The ten-day solitary confinement was finished and Breed was allowed to return to the work details. Broken fortunes were with Breed. His first duty sergeant was Sergeant Fitz. Fitz took up where he had left off, bullying and harassing Breed. At 0500 sharp Fitz was at the stockade. As the day progressed Breed grew more determined and Fitz sensed the futility of his efforts. Breed had not eaten since reveille, yet he maintained a steady pace. Fitz saved the water detail for last knowing Breed would be thirsty. The gamble failed. Breed continued to work much to Fitz's dismay. Fitz ladled a dipper of water, drank deeply, and poured the remainder over his head, then shook like a dog. The water momentarily blinded him. Breed stepped forward and filled the dipper. Fitz cleared his eye and moved to intercept Breed. With casual disdain Breed poured the water over Fitz's boots and threw the ladle into the bucket. "Thanks anyway, Fitz. I'm not thirsty."

"Fine with me," Fitz replied as he struggled to stifle his rage. "I'll have another drink."

Fitz returned Breed to the stockade. Strange, Breed thought. We're done early. The next guard watch won't be set. He could not pinpoint his misgivings but Fitz was up to something. Breed became wary, tense in anticipation of the unexpected. As Fitz unlocked the inside passage of the stockade, Breed stood well off to one side. Fitz then unlocked Breed's cell. Breed gave him wide berth as he stepped into the dark cell. In an instant Breed was smothered with a blanket and collapsed under the combined weight of three men. Instinctively he doubled up to protect his stomach and groin. He covered his head with both hands. The blows and kicks pummeled his body with stunning fury. Pain exploded in his ear then his face. An electric jolt seared his rib cage. Bits and pieces of conversation faded to be replaced by the thunderous pounding of his heart. Slowly he lost his grip on consciousness and faded into darkness.

"I'm here," Breed mumbled. A soft voice pierced the darkness.

"Breed," the voice continued to call his name. "Please talk to me. It's Josie. Please," she pleaded.

He attempted to open his eyes and succeeded in cracking the left one. He saw Josie's blurred image leaning over him. "I can't see you clearly. Help me sit up." As he moved, shock waves of pain shot through his body. Josie faded and he slipped once again into blessed blackness.

Sometime during the night he regained consciousness. Sawbones was propped against the wall, snoring like a sow. Breed surveyed his surroundings with one eye. He gingerly felt his face. The effort made his bruised body hurt. His right eye felt like a ripe tomato. Further inspection revealed a taped nose and a cracked and split lower lip. "All the pieces are there," Sawbones's voice startled him. "Slightly rearranged but nonetheless there."

"You could have fooled me, Doc. Will I live?" Breed laughed, and his side rebelled in sharp pain. "Oh, that hurts," he whispered.

"It should. You have several cracked or broken ribs."

"Why am I hearing bells? My ear is ringing."

"You've been kicked there. It will be cauliflowered for a few days and tender as hell." The doc looked at him and shook his head. "Add to the list a swollen eye, sore ribs, and a partially broken nose."

"Sounds good to me. Is that all?" Breed laughed, then

moaned. "What the hell is a partially broken nose?"

"Ah, it's off to one side a touch but you can breathe through both ports." The doc smiled. "You should see the old man. He's stomping mad. Says this can't happen on his fort." The doc looked seriously at Breed. "I suppose you'll tell him you walked into a door?"

Breed remained silent, then spoke. "Let me know if you get a couple of soldiers in with bruised hands or busted feet. I owe them a return favor."

"Sure thing." The doc covered his rising anger well. To the doctor, wounded men were duty, but to patch up a soldier hurt by malicious intent was another matter. "Now that you are awake I want to do something about your eye. I'm going to make a small cut underneath the lower lid and drain it."

The following days were a mixture of pain and extreme discomfort. Breed's cracked ribs gradually healed but he had many sleepless nights and tender days. Anticipation of a dreaded sneeze was as bad as the actual event. His swollen eye had discolored into a beautiful jet black and deep, rich purple.

Josie was Breed's strength. She brought him delicious home-cooked meals in the infirmary. He was convinced she was using her father's influence to get meat, eggs, and vegetables. Although Josie did not appear to be going hungry, Breed knew he was eating her food. His confinements in the stockade and now in the infirmary had worn thin. The approaching thirty-day appeal gave him little hope. He became depressed. Josie saw what was happening and fought against it.

Her spunky attitude gave him a much-needed boost. With Josie's pleading, and arm-twisting from Sawbones, Breed was allowed a daily walk. Under escort. Breed, Josie, and the armed guard walked the inside perimeter of the fort. These walks gave Breed a release from confinement. Josie's company was pure delight.

Stills stopped by when he could to jaw. Breed enjoyed talking with the trooper because he was privy to the latest gossip. "Care to know who pounded on your head?" he asked with a smile. "It will cost you a future favor," Dave kidded him.

"I can't pay you a penny now. You are looking at a man without rank or privilege."

"We'll settle later," Dave acknowledged. "Rumor has it Fitz bought Gowen and Simmons along with Corporal Calhoun. Five bucks each."

"How did you find out?" Breed was curious to know.

"Simmons got drunk with his five dollars and bragged too much."

"Simmons is a cheap bastard," Breed said in disgust. "He's like some hussy sellin' to the highest bidder."

"Want me to haul them over here so you can even the score?"

"You're joking." Breed laughed. "I am at the mercy of the flies at the moment. The right time will come."

"The new rifle shipment is due tomorrow," Dave reminded Breed. "They'll be stored in the new armory. Under heavy guard."

"I wish them better luck this time," Breed commented with bitterness.

Breed was preoccupied with the news of the rifles. He was convinced Fitz would make a move. Stills mentioned the rifles were to be sent south to help General Clemments. Breed couldn't control his mounting concern and asked Dave to have Alcorn stop by the infirmary.

First Sergeant Alcorn stopped by and rehashed their plan. Alcorn would have to get the rifles as soon as they arrived. Breed suggested to the sergeant to double the guard detail for the armory. Alcorn told him of the special detail and extra precautions. None of these measures reassured Breed. Something would go wrong. He was to return to the stockade tomorrow from the infirmary. This served to deepen his gloom.

Sergeant Fitz had not suffered from the investigation that followed the theft of the rifles. He knew he was covered, his alibis solid. There were no loose ends. Corporal Calhoun was bought and wouldn't squeal. The spoiled child of fortune, Fitz, was blessed again. The location of the new armory was located over an old drainage ditch. Fitz had worked on the detail that planked the ditch with logs and covered it with fill dirt. If the soldiers who built the new armory had gone six inches deeper, they would have struck the planks, and changed the location.

After a lengthy late-night search Fitz discovered the drainage ditch outside the fort's wall. Corporal Calhoun and Fitz spent a long night working together and mucked out a cramped tunnel which led under the new armory. They sawed through the floor planks and shored them from below. The floor appeared solid. Fitz had known the arrival date of the rifles for several weeks; his paid contact had listed the date. The rifles arrived two days later. Fitz had a grace period before the rifles were to be shipped to General Clemments. The sergeant had doubled his price for the rifles. They were worth more. Lacy had screamed like a mashed cat but agreed to the asking price.

Fitz walked away from the bustle of early morning activity around the armory. The rifles had arrived safely and were under lock and key. Corporal Calhoun fell in beside Fitz and matched his stride. "I've been meaning to speak with you about a certain business matter, Sergeant Fitz," Calhoun needled him. "Thinking real serious about our eighty-twenty split. It ain't fair. Maybe we ought to split it even. Fifty-fifty."

"Why, you . . ." Fitz seethed at first, then smiled. He had long anticipated this possibility. "Tell me what's on your mind, Corporal?"

"I've been doin' equal work. I want equal pay." A smug grin touched his face.

"Fine idea, Calhoun." Fitz beamed as he put his arm around the corporal's shoulder. "Let's go eat, partner, and we'll talk business." Corporal Calhoun was too pleased with himself to realize he had made a fatal error in judgment.

The two men sat by themselves in the dining hall and discussed their plan in hushed voices. "It's a go tonight. We'll meet after your midnight watch in the stockade." Fitz strung Calhoun along without the younger man ever the wiser. "I'll come and get you and we'll move the rifles. How's that sound, partner?"

Corporal Calhoun grinned like a possum. He was no longer one of Fitz's boys. He was a full-fledged equal. His pappy had told him, "Be your own man. Don't let people push you around." Well, I finally made it. Calhoun's thoughts were high-mettled. What Robert E. Lee Calhoun hadn't learned from his pappy was that the Fitzes of this world readily devoured the Calhoun.

With a cool evening breeze in his face, Fitz was happy, almost jovial. All the pieces were falling into place. Calhoun would have to go, no doubt about it. The corporal's stockade duty might provide the opportunity. Fitz pondered the endless possibilities as he walked toward the bulletin board. Shouts of joy and congratulations echoed in the air. As Fitz approached, several men rushed to him. "Nice going, Sarge. You're our new first sergeant." The big Irishman basked in the prestige of the promotion.

"Thanks, boys. I'll take real good care of you now."

One of the nearby soldiers commented to his friend, "In a pig's eye. Just means he's got a bigger head than before." The other soldier spoke as they watched Fitz. "Look at him, higher than a Georgia pine. We're all gonna pay for that promotion."

Shouldering his way through the happy crowd Fitz headed straight for the old man's office. "You done a fine job for a dumb 'Mick' nobody gave a damn about. Yes, sir. First Sergeant Fitzpatrick. I like it. Got a nice ring." Fitz wanted to thank Colonel Prentice while rubbing salt in old wounds. Savoring his own cunning Fitz bounded lightly onto the porch. Just then Josie stepped out of the colonel's office. Damn, Fitz cursed. She is the last person I wanted to see.

"Evening, Miss Prentice." Fitz hoped she would settle for the usual formalities.

"You blackguard. Don't sweet-talk me," Josie snapped at him. "You might hoodwink Daddy but you haven't fooled me."

"I don't understand," Fitz mockingly apologized.

"You, Sergeant, and I use the term loosely, have some evil hold over my father. I intend to find what it is and put a stop to it. If I were a man, I would beat that evil out of you." Josie was mad, breathing hard.

"Calm yourself, please." Fitz stepped forward and touched her arm. Josie recoiled as if his touch burned.

"Don't you ever touch me," she hissed.

Josie's anger unsettled Fitz and stirred inside him deeply rooted fears of discovery. He icily stared at her. She met his eyes and held the look.

"I can't understand you—" She cut him short.

"I'll hear no more from you. Remember, I will break your evil hold if it's the last thing I do."

Yes, ma'am, he thought as he stepped aside. It might well be the last thing you ever do. "Excuse me, miss. I'm here to see the colonel."

Josie turned on her heel and strode angrily away. She reflected on her conversation with Fitz and felt she had been too brash. No! He deserved it. I won't shy away.

She returned to the cottage knowing she would have to help her father home later that night. Her attempts to learn more about Sergeant Fitz had dead-ended. The men were reluctant to talk with her. She was a woman as well as the commanding officer's daughter. The soldiers also appeared to be fearful of Sergeant Fitz. She bitterly recognized her lack of progress toward the solution of her father's decline and fall.

CHAPTER
9

Josie returned after midnight to her father's office. As she feared, he had passed out. She quietly straightened the stack of papers and books strewn about his desk. A crumpled piece of paper clutched in her father's hand caught Josie's eye. She pried his fingers apart and took the paper. It was a handwritten message torn roughly in half. She read the portion.

Captain Prentice
Where in the hell
for your reinforcements
you join my command
your presence. Report to

As Josie studied the paper the door opened, whisper-quiet. She glanced to see who had come in at this late hour. While Sergeant Fitz closed the door, she discreetly tucked the note in her apron pocket. Josie felt uneasy as the big Irishman approached the desk. "May I be of assistance, Miss Prentice?" Fitz's charm was unsettling. Josie neither moved nor spoke. She was at a loss how to respond. "Is he all right, Miss Prentice?" Fitz stood beside her and glanced at the colonel.

As Josie followed Fitz's eyes, he hit her flush on the chin, knocking her out. He caught her as she fell. Effortlessly Fitz scooped Josie into his arms, blew out the lantern, and walked to the door. He cracked it wide enough to peek out. Nothing moved. Fitz stayed in the shadows and carried Josie to the break in the log wall. With the logs temporarily removed from behind the old armory, Fitz eased Josie through the hole and laid her on the ground. Fitz then squeezed his bulk out the hole. He hoisted Josie onto his shoulder and worked around the wall perimeter. At the drainage ditch he bound and gagged her with strips of petticoat then left her tied to a log inside the mouth of the tunnel.

Corporal Calhoun was on stockade guard duty. He sat in a vegetative state at the front desk and absent-mindedly cleaned his fingernails with a pocketknife. A brass key dangled from the loop on the knife handle. The cells were behind him down a narrow corridor. Calhoun idly looked up as Fitz stepped inside the confining room. "You by yourself, Calhoun?" Fitz asked as he scanned the room and corridor.

"Yep, Sarge. Only me and your friend in the back," he answered smartly.

"Good. We can't be seen together before this next caper." Fitz lowered his voice. "We're going to set up

Stalwart and you are gonna play a major role in doing it."

"How, Fitz?" Calhoun dropped his chair down on all four legs, his interest aroused.

Fitz wandered around the office as he talked to the corporal. "In due time, lad. You'll be the first to know." Fitz grinned at the unsuspecting young man. The sarge spotted a pair of leg shackles hanging from a wall hook. He removed the length of chain and subconsciously jerked on it as if to test its strength. Calhoun watched him in silence.

"You any happier about me becoming an equal partner?" Calhoun stupidly asked.

"I'm rightly pleased, Calhoun." Fitz lied graciously. "Can't see no reason why we shouldn't split fifty-fifty, partner. I'll do the figurin', so you won't have a care about that." The corporal nodded agreeably.

Calhoun relaxed noticeably and returned to cleaning his fingernails. Fitz casually sauntered behind him, then violently threw his weight against the chair. Calhoun was pinned tight to the heavy oak desk, arms trapped against his chest, breath knocked out. Fitz looped the chain around Calhoun's neck like a garrote and jerked the chain tight. His thick biceps bulged, the tendons in his beefy forearms strained with the effort. Corporal Robert E. Lee Calhoun, stunned from the blow and breathless, was quickly strangled. The corporal's feet tapped a rapid death staccato on the wooden floor as Fitz struggled to keep the chain tight. The foot beat gradually slowed in tempo, then ceased altogether. Mindful not to release the pressure, Fitz twisted the chain so it would not slip. He yanked the corporal upright and dragged him to the door that separated the office from the cells. Fitz used his shoulder to hold Calhoun upright while he passed one of the ends through the barred window and hanged Calhoun. When Fitz opened the door wide, Calhoun was hidden from view. A smile crossed Fitz's flushed face. "Now, partner. We have a new pay split. One hundred percent for me. *Nada* for you."

Fitz hustled to the desk, grabbed the key ring, and walked into the interior of the stockade. He tenderfooted to Breed's cell and peeked through the barred door. The hallway lantern cast sufficient light to show Breed was asleep on his cot. Fitz opened the flap on his holster and pulled out his .45. With nary a sound he unlocked the door and stepped back as it swung open. Breed had not stirred. Fitz tiptoed in and smacked Breed's exposed side. Breed jerked awake and blindly lashed out at the source of pain. His clubbing fist hit Fitz solidly in the chest and knocked him into the wall. As Fitz slid to the floor, Breed crouched on his knees, ready to dive on the fallen man. The loud *click* of the hammer being cocked put a halt to that notion. "One move and you're dead," snarled Fitz. The force of Breed's blow had stunned him. "Do as I say or you'll die here."

Breed had not moved. The flow of adrenaline had been replaced with a dull pain. He gently rubbed his side. "You're pretty good at hitting people when they're down, Fitz," Breed ragged him. "You probably hit women, too."

"Shut up," Fitz ordered. "Get your boots on and head for the door."

"This unexpected generosity doesn't fit, Fitz," Breed commented sarcastically. "You're up to something."

"Let's just say it's all part of the game plan and you are the key player."

"What's to stop me from walking out the door and going straight to the old man's office?"

"Nothing. First of all, Colonel Prentice does as I say." Fitz let that sink in. "Then you'll have to answer some questions about the health of your jailer, Corporal Calhoun. Try and explain the whereabouts of Miss Prentice to the grieving father." Fitz smiled confidently. "Go for the explanation of the missing rifles and why your hat was so carelessly left behind. Looks like a closed case to me." Fitz laughed at the stacked odds.

"Nicely done, Fitz, I'll give you credit. Unless you kill me, you know I'll come looking for you."

"Oh, I'm so scared." He feigned horror. "An escaped criminal, kidnapper, and murderer. Why, every bounty hunter, lawman, and soldier this side of the Pecos will be searchin' for your worthless hide. Get going. Out through the hole behind the old armory."

Fitz motioned toward the door with his pistol. Breed did as he was told. The Irishman followed at a cautious distance. "Hold it right there," Fitz ordered as he turned the lantern down. "I'd just as soon shoot you as look at you, so stay put." Breed glanced to the side and saw Calhoun's boots sticking out from behind the door.

Fitz crossed to the front door and prudently opened it. He checked outside. Breed was close enough to the desk to pocket Calhoun's knife and key. Fitz snapped his head back inside. "Git," he ordered, and stepped clear of the door. "And good luck," he added with a sardonic smile.

Breed guardedly approached the door. He wondered if he was walking into a setup. Nothing moved as he stepped outside. The night was inky black and he moved slowly toward the armory. Breed doubted Fitz's word about the wall being open. It was too risky. Those doubts were rudely laid to rest by the hard steel pistol barrel that prodded his spine. "The hole. Go for it," whispered Fitz. "I'll be right behind you." He laughed softly. "Think of it. A hero. I shot the prisoner as he tried to escape."

Breed ducked between the logs and crawled away from the wall. He could hear Fitz replacing the logs. What do I do now? Breed wondered. Run? No, he would stop that traitorous Irishman. Fitz had made a good point, though. Lawmen would be as thick as ticks on a south Texas steer looking for him. The bounty hunters would be like wildflowers after a wet spring, everywhere. Gun-running would turn the veteran soldiers against him with a vengeance. The odds told him to hightail it, but Fitz had slandered his name and reputation. Breed's anger mounted as he mulled over the events of the evening. Fitz's words sank in with deadly finality: Josie's kidnapping, Calhoun's murder, and the missing rifles.

The new armory. It was so blatantly obvious Breed had overlooked it. He would go around to the opposite wall and scale it by the powder magazine. No-Feet used it on his nighttime forays. Breed's progress was agonizingly slow as he traveled by touch. He heard the steps of the sentries as they paced the catwalk. Rounding the corner Breed heard muffled voices and recognized Fitz's brogue.

"Pay up, Lacy. Sixty gold pieces for the rifles. I gave you the ammo as a bonus." Fitz sounded pleased with his good deed.

"Ya know what, Fitz? It rubs my ass like a saddle sore—"

"Cut the song and dance, Lacy," Fitz interrupted. "Pay or take a hike, choice's yours."

"Here's your filthy money, Mick." Lacy spat out the words as he threw a small leather pouch at Fitz's feet.

"It's dirty money, considering the source. You." Fitz checked his burning desire to snatch Lacy off his horse and bust his smart mouth. Instead he felt for the pouch.

"Ain't you gonna count it?"

"Nope. If it's short I'll pass word to Walking Tall or Campesino. They'll settle any loose ends," Fitz calmly told Lacy.

"Meet you at the logjam. Have the rest of the ammo with ya," Lacy instructed as he turned and disappeared into the night.

"Gowen," Fitz called softly.

"Ya," came the response from the catwalk.

"We're done. Get lost," Fitz ordered.

"Right, Sarge. I'm gone."

Breed remained in a squatting position until convinced Fitz was gone. He stood and stretched his cramped thigh muscles. The sound of a horse sent him to the ground. He saw the vague silhouette of Fitz as he rode away from the fort, a bundle draped over the rear of the horse. The ground beneath Breed suddenly gave way and he tumbled down the bank. As he brushed himself off, a damp whisper of a breeze chilled him as it gently blew from the hole in the bank. A tunnel! I should have guessed it. As Breed crawled cautiously into the opening, he knocked a small box of matches from a support brace. Breed worked his way further into the moist tunnel, then struck the match. His cupped hand shielded the flickering flame. He was at the elbow of a vertical shaft that led up to the sawn floor planks of the new armory. A small candle stub had been left on a plank. Breed lit the wick, stood through the hole in the planks. Pilfered rifle and ammo boxes littered the floor.

"If I'm caught here, I'm dead," Breed talked underbreath. The unknown fear that one of Fitz's cronies might have sounded the alarm, or perchance someone had discovered Calhoun, spurred Breed's departure. As he ducked into the shaft, he saw his battered Stetson where Fitz had said it would be. Beside the brim was a piece of torn petticoat. "Why, that bastard," Breed swore. "I'm sure as hell going to ruin his plans now."

Breed plopped his hat on his head, stuffed the petticoat rag into a pocket, and slipped down the shaft. Fitz hadn't labored too hard to get the rifles. His plan had worked to perfection due in large part to its simplicity. Breed snuffed the candle and crawled out of the tunnel. The night air chilled him. He suddenly remembered the bundle on Fitz's horse. "Josie. I must be losing my mind." The time in the stockade and infirmary had dulled his senses. He felt brain-dead. "Damn, I'll need a rifle." He cursed his oversight and headed back into the tunnel. When he emerged several minutes later he carried a .45-70 carbine and two pockets full of shells.

Breed purposefully slow-paced himself. He realized not to push too hard or he would never make it to the logjam. His arms ached from the weight of the carbine. Shifting it from hand to hand helped. The loose shells pounded painfully against his sore ribs and prevented him from going faster. He stumbled and fell headlong onto the grassy field. His legs trembled and thigh muscles begged for a rest. He knew what a wind-broke horse felt like. The sweet smell of pine told him he was close to the ponderosa stand. Breed pushed ahead, his tired body resisting the continued punishment. Minutes later he was confronted by a solid wall of trees and scrub underbrush. He had hunted here in the past and should have spotted the logging road that cut through the trees. A black, featureless mass challenged him. It was now a matter of choice as to which direction to follow.

Breed's gut feeling was to bear to the right. He trotted slowly and searched for anything recognizable. Despair edged into his mind and cast doubts on the wisdom of his choice. "Be rational. Walk for one thousand paces," he reassured himself. Breed counted by tens, then hundreds. Frustration cut at him but also spurred him on. At eight hundred paces the black forest still defied him. Nine fifty, nothing. As he counted the last twenty paces, he fell into a grassy dip, stumbled forward over a small ridge, and landed in another dip. "That's it"—his exhaustion was cut by excitement— "the logging road from the logjam."

Fort Manning had been built using timber from this stand. The log skidders used by the lumberjacks had left deep wheel ruts in the grassy meadow. The logjam was named for the big pile of logs that had broken loose from their skidders and tumbled into a draw.

A haunting silence slapped Breed in the face. The logjam was deserted, he was too late. He slumped exhausted against a tree. Fitz's deep rumbling laugh brought Breed to his feet. A slight breeze carried a mixture of voices from below. Breed angled silently down the grassy slope and spotted a small fire in the bottom of the draw. A group of men were tightly clustered around the flickering flames. "I'll even give you a bonus, Lacy." Fitz laughed again and disappeared into the darkness. Lacy waited, not knowing what to expect. Fitz returned into the circle of light and pushed Josie toward the cowboy. "You can have her for nothin'."

Lacy's eyes lighted up with pleasure; a low whistle left his lips. The cowboy could scarcely believe his luck. He hadn't been with a woman for several months and Fitz was giving him this young lady. "What's the catch, Fitz?" Lacy questioned. "Nobody gives no one like this away for nothin'."

"Let's just say she was my insurance. Now that I don't need her, she's yours."

"Hot damn," Lacy muttered as he moved beside Josie. He licked his lips as he feasted his eyes on her body. Lacy wrapped his arms around her and bodily carried her to the fire. Josie flailed her legs wildly. To no avail. Her eyes burned with hatred that masked a deep fear. "Well, ain't she a fine-lookin' gal," Lacy spoke as he traced her chin with his rough fingers. Josie jerked her head away, her skin crawling at his touch. "Feisty, too. I like that in a woman."

Josie was rooted to the spot with fear. Her stomach turned at his touch. She fought back the urge to scream, or worse yet, to faint. Lacy stood in front of her and reached out to unfasten the top button of her blouse. Josie stepped back slightly and smiled. Lacy paused and dropped his fingers to the next button. Josie took advantage of his hesitation and kneed him solidly between the legs. A shocked look twisted Lacy's face before he doubled over in excruciating pain.

Fitz leaped forward and slapped Josie hard across the face. "You dumb bitch. He'll kill you for that."

The two other men sitting around the fire, Dwight and Lloyd Willitts, watched the episode with a great deal of amusement. Dwight was sipping a cup of coffee when Lacy doubled over and dropped to the ground. He laughed, then choked on the coffee and spewed it over himself and his cousin.

"What in the hell is so danged blamed funny?" Lloyd asked as he wiped the coffee off the side of his face.

Dwight coughed out the coffee from his throat and managed to talk. "Ain't it a shame. Lacy finally gets a woman and look what happens."

"Ya, I see what you mean." Lloyd joined him in laughter. "I sure know one thing he won't be doing tonight." They laughed so hard they doubled over as Lacy moaned and tucked tighter into a ball.

"Maybe we ought to help poor ol' Lacy out." Dwight smiled and got to his feet.

"It's the least we can do for a friend," Lloyd volunteered as he stepped toward Josie.

Breed laid the .45-70 across a log and sighted on the coffeepot. A slight breeze fanned the coals into flickering flames. Breed gently pulled the trigger. The thunderous clap of the shot reverberated off the narrow sides of the draw. The coffeepot disintegrated. The Willittses lunged away from the steaming coals as they drew their pistols. Lacy, in pain and unable to stand, crawled into the darkness. Fitz's attempt to reach Josie was stopped by Breed's next shot, which sent him sprawling for cover.

"This is Captain Drake," Breed hollered at the men. "You are surrounded. Throw down your weapons."

The reply was a blistering fusillade of shots. Breed could hear the slugs zip past or hit the tree trunk with solid thuds. He shot at the cousins, reloaded, and shot at Lacy. "Move down, men. Flank them," Breed shouted as he slid downhill to the left. He came to rest behind another log and shot again. As he slipped along the log he fired several more shots. He was hoping to fool Fitz into thinking there were many soldiers trying to capture them. The volume of fire died. Breed could not see any of the gunmen. The coals were out. He heard voices, probably the Willittses helping Lacy. Breed cocked his head to help pinpoint the location before he shot. Answering shots probed the darkness. Josie's scream pierced the night. Breed dared not shoot for fear of hitting her.

"You'll pay for this, Fitz," Lacy groaned. "You're a double-dealin' bastard."

"Horseshit, Lacy," answered Fitz. "Probably some of your riffraff friends trying to square up one of your underhanded deals. Take the girl. That should make us even."

"I've got her. I won't forget this," Lacy threatened.

"Big deal." Fitz brushed aside the threat. "Try to enjoy yourself tonight. If you can," Fitz threw that in to spite Lacy.

Fading hoofbeats deserted Breed. He had lost everything on his gamble. Josie was gone. The rifles were on their way out of here, and Fitz was still on the loose. Breed couldn't bear the thought of Josie at the mercy of Lacy or the Willittses. He slipped out from behind the log and hiked up to the logging road. He would find No-Feet. Together they would track those three and get Josie back safely.

167

CHAPTER
_10_

After Breed returned from the logjam, he sneaked into the fort, and rousted No-Feet. Together they set out to track and follow Lacy and the others. An hour past sunup No-Feet knew that Lacy, Josie, and the Willittses were headed for the Mexican town of Dos Diablos. The dusty, dirty pueblo was inside the ill-defined Mexican border, and the last watering hole before El Desierto Grande de Chihuahua.

"Can we beat them there?" Breed questioned the silent Indian.

The Apache said nothing. He continued to watch the labored progress of the three horses, four riders, and two pack burros. "Yes, we'll be in the town first. They travel with too many rifles. And the doubled woman slows the horse."

Breed and No-Feet rode cautiously from the mesa, heedful not to raise telltale dust. They walked their horses across loose scree fields. On the desert floor they rode hard with knowledge of two springs ahead of them. This was No-Feet's country. He knew it like the back of his hand. Their horses were watered and fresh when they bypassed the bandit pueblo of Mesquital. The town, indistinguishable from the sur-rounding desert, was home for many border raiders. This was lawless country. Neither the United States government nor the Mexican government had the manpower or the willpower to clean out the town.

An hour's ride beyond Mesquital, No-Feet slacked off and Breed rode alongside. "We go on?" the Apache asked.

"Why do you ask? We will arrive before those gun-runners, won't we?"

No-Feet nodded. "From here on we face the *Rurales*. If they catch us, we die here."

"We knew that when we started," Breed answered with determination.

Dos Diablos was an insult of a town. The main street, crudely cobbled, was fronted by twenty houses. They looked alike, made from the same dirt that constantly blew and swirled through the town. An open sewer ran down the middle of the street, further fouling the already wretched air. At the end of the street stood a whitewashed adobe church. Its single spire rose above the high walls of the church's inner courtyard. The town's sole cantina, La Posa, was across the street from the church. In the cantina you took your chances with the food and washed it down with cheap rotgut. The local *pulque* was deadly.

Breed and No-Feet circled Dos Diablos and rode in from the south. No-Feet cautiously approached the rear of the cantina as Breed covered him. The Apache went on foot to check the bar and town. He returned and told Breed both were clear. Taking his .45-70 with him, Breed followed the Indian inside the cantina. They took a table in the corner. The Mexican proprietor came forward. *"Señores, a sus ordenes."*

"Almuerso y dos cervezas, por favor," Breed ordered.
"La sopa del dia, tambien, señor?"
"Si, porsupuesto."
"We eat fast," No-Feet spoke after the man left them. "Those four will be here soon."

They ate in silence; both listened and watched for the arrival of Lacy and company. Breed smiled fleetingly at the thought of a third devil name for this town. The food. He was skittish to ask what kind of meat was in the soup. The lack of stray dogs might have provided the clue. Nevertheless Breed and No-Feet ate heartily. They were famished after the long ride.

A small patio sided the cantina. Four tables were sheltered from the blistering sun by a thatched roof. Half a dozen large water filled ollas hung from the vigas. They cooled the shaded patio while more inside kept the cantina surprisingly pleasant.

The clatter of shod horses on the cobblestone brought Breed and No-Feet to their feet. The proprietor sensed trouble and deftly plucked liquor bottles from the shelf behind the bar and stashed them beneath the counter. He hastily cleared the table and disappeared into the kitchen. Breed stepped through a tattered curtain into the dark storage room. No-Feet slipped behind the counter as the clatter ceased. The men stopped beside the patio, dismounted, and tied their horses to the corner post. They sought the patio shade. Josie remained seated on the rump of Lacy's horse.

"Get down or I'll knock you offa there," he snapped at her.

Josie glared defiantly at him as she slipped off the horse. She knew full well Lacy would do as he said. Her hands were tied together with a leather strap. The right side of her face was swollen, a dark purple bruise under her right eye. Lacy motioned her to sit at one of the tables. Breed watched Lacy through the curtain and smiled to see how tenderly he walked and sat.

"Oye, patron. Quatro cervezas. Pronto," Lacy rudely shouted.

The Mexican emerged from the kitchen carrying four clay mugs of beer. He was disinclined to go into the patio. Breed parted the curtain with his rifle barrel and motioned him to put the mugs down and leave. No-Feet unbuckled his pistol belt and stuck the .45 in his waistband. He covered it with his shirt. The Apache grabbed the beers and walked outside. He placed the mugs on the table in silence.

"Hey, you," Dwight spoke to No-Feet. "You Mexican?" The Apache ignored him. "Speak to me, Injun. I'm talkin' to you." Dwight became hostile. No-Feet did not speak as he finished placing the beer around the table.

"Lay off him, man." Lloyd grabbed Dwight's arm. "He's just a dumb Injun. Leave him be."

Dwight stared at No-Feet, looking him over real close. "I don't like you," growled Dwight. "Hey, dummy, get us something to eat." The cowboy pointed to his mouth, then toward the kitchen.

No-Feet returned inside the cantina. Breed was out of the storage room and stood next to the window. The

Apache glanced at Breed and received the go-ahead nod. The Indian went into the kitchen for a tray of tortillas, ground peppers, and utensils. He removed his .45, cocked it, and placed it in his hand. He covered the pistol with a wiping rag and carried the tray to the patio.

Dwight and Lloyd were arguing. Both were hot.

"I'm tellin' you, I've seen that Injun someplace before," Dwight insisted as he eyeballed No-Feet.

"You been out in the sun too long, Dwight," Lloyd reasoned with his cousin. "Who in the hell knows we're here? Answer me that? Nobody."

"Guess you're right, but I still don't like him."

Luck was with No-Feet. As he neared Josie, she raised her mug with both hands to sip the beer. The Apache stepped close and clipped her arm. Beer spilled down her front. She stood quickly and dropped her mug. "Oh, I'm all wet," she complained as she wiped her dress.

This was all No-Feet needed. Josie was safely out of the line of fire. No-Feet turned on the seated men. "Anybody moves, I'll shoot. Let her go."

Lloyd and Lacy sat speechless as the Apache spoke. The meaning of his words slowly dawned on them.

Dwight lurched to his feet. "Says you—" was all he got out as he drew his pistol. No-Feet shot him. The .45 slug hit Dwight flush in the chest and staggered him away from the table. The cowboy hit a low retaining wall and backflipped out of the patio. No-Feet leapt off to one side and hit Josie as he hurtled past. She sprawled to the earthen floor. Lloyd snapped out of his trance, drew his pistol, and took aim at the Indian.

Breed, .45-70 already shouldered, filled the front sights with Lloyd's blue shirt and squeezed off the round. The bullet hit Lloyd below his left armpit, wreaked havoc on its brutal smash through his body, and exited from his right shoulder. Lloyd momentarily remained on his feet, then crumpled. Lacy, unable to locate the second shot, mistakenly dived for shelter through the cantina door. He'd barely cleared the frame when No-Feet shot him. The impact propelled Lacy inside the room. As he instinctively struggled to his feet, Breed shot him. The blow spun Lacy completely around and left him dead, facedown on the floor.

Josie sat on the dirt floor of the patio, a dazed expression frozen on her face. Within the last ten seconds three men had died at her feet. None of it made sense to her. No-Feet warily approached and checked the cousins to make certain they were dead. Breed cautiously toed Lacy onto his back and knew at a glance the cowboy was dead. As Breed stepped onto the patio, Josie looked at him in complete disbelief. She couldn't comprehend the sight of a friend. With tears in her eyes, she struggled to her feet, and tried to hug Breed. The leather strap held her hands tightly together.

"Breed," she whispered, "I can't believe . . ." No-Feet handed Breed his knife and he cut the strap. Josie fell against his chest and wept. The violence of the shootout had unnerved her. Breed held her tightly and stroked her with a firm hand.

"Try and calm yourself." His deep voice steadied her. "I know it won't be easy. Put them out of your mind."

"Breed, they're such awful men. Crude and ugly." She grimaced. "Momma would be unhappy with me for saying this, but I'm glad they're dead. Could we leave this place?" she begged. "It frightens me. Please?"

"I know how you feel. Go with No-Feet. Our horses are around back." He pointed her in the right direction. "I'll take care of this."

Breed dragged the bodies behind the cantina, and kicked dirt over the bloody dirt floor. He rifled their pockets and took a thick wad of pesos from Lacy and smaller wads from the Willittses. Breed unbuckled their pistol belts and took their pistols. No-Feet put them in Breed's saddlebag.

"Get one of their horses for Josie," Breed told No-Feet. "I'll be out in a shake." Breed ducked inside the cantina. Minutes later he hurried out and swung onto his horse.

"What about those three?" Josie asked. "Do we leave them?"

"For fifty pesos they'll get a proper burial," Breed replied brusquely. "As a matter of fact, the *patron* seemed relieved. I gather they were regular customers. Let's ride."

They rode with haste through the deserted streets. The clatter of the hooves was deafening. On the rare occasions Breed had been in nameless towns like Dos Diablos, he had never seen the town's people. Doors were closed and windows shuttered. He wondered if anyone lived here. Looking past the stilled houses he viewed the distant mountains, which shimmered invitingly. Beyond these mountains lay safety.

"Josie, our lives depend upon your answer to my question. What did Lacy do with the rifles?"

"What rifles?" she replied in honest ignorance.

"Damn it," Breed barked. "Didn't each of the Willittses lead a pack burro?" Breed probed impatiently.

"Oh, those," she answered. "We stopped after sunrise. Lacy left me tied to his horse. The three men walked a short distance and met with some peasants." Josie continued to detail the exchange. "I could hear them talking but not well enough to understand the words. Besides, Lacy told me if I looked he'd kill me then and there. They returned in high spirits talking about their deal. From there we rode straight for Dos Diablos. You know the rest."

"Where did you stop. Do you remember anything?" Breed needed answers.

She shook her head. "No."

"Las Cruces? Jimenez or Madera?" Breed named the closest towns to the route Lacy had taken.

"I don't know, Breed," Josie apologized. "They all look alike. Wait! One of the towns had a church with twin spires. I remember hearing the bells toll as I waited for Lacy."

"Mesquital." Breed breathed a sigh of relief. "I should have thought of it."

"Why do you need to know?"

"It's Campesino's town. Now we know who bought the rifles." Breed explained his reasons for needing the information. "We'll steer clear of it. It does make sense, though. Close to the border and secure. The *Federales* seldom get up there."

Dos Diablos dwindled in the distance as Breed, Josie, and No-Feet reached the safety of the foothills. Their horses loped easily as they sensed the danger had passed.

"Promise me one thing, Breed," Josie jokingly requested. "Never let me come this way again. Ever."

"It's a deal." He smiled. "I feel the same way."

Breed and Josie were preoccupied in playful banter. When No-Feet stopped, neither Breed nor Josie noticed. Suddenly Josie reined in to avoid a collision with the Apache. Breed abruptly quit his chitchat and immediately searched the hills. Two flanking columns of dust closed in from the front. A large cloud behind cut off escape to the rear.

"How could they know?" Breed asked in disbelief. "We were the only ones in town."

"I don't know." Josie didn't understand what Breed meant.

"Our damned cursed luck. The *Federales,*" Breed said dejectedly. "Damned if they don't know everything that goes on around here."

"The who?" Josie blindly asked.

"*Federales Rurales.* Sort of the Mexican army. They are a power unto themselves. What the banditos don't rule or take, these guys do."

"Can't we outrun them?" Josie questioned. The look on Breed's face told her it was an impossibility.

"We wouldn't make it a mile. Our only way out is to talk. Wish me luck," Breed jested. "I'm going to need it."

Breed and Josie dismounted and sat on the ground in the shade of their horses. No-Feet remained seated on his pony as the columns converged. Each flank had five riders, and the main body included ten riders and the commanding officer. As the riders closed in, Josie scoffed at their ragtag appearance, which falsely belittled their professionalism. No uniforms were visible, rather a medley of tattered, weathered shirts, torn and mended pants. Wide-brimmed sombreros shaded each rider. By sharp contrast their horses were excellent stock, well cared for and smartly groomed. The soldiers rode like they had been weaned in their ornately decorated and hand-crafted saddles. Their pistols and rifles were clean, oiled, and well used. Seldom did anyone outrun these soldiers. Breed was relieved he hadn't entertained the thought. The *Federales* surrounded the trio, blocking all escape.

The commanding officer rode forward. He matched every movement of the jet-black stud, which stood a good seventeen hands high. The man was solid, about Breed's age. His face was Spanish, a thin Roman nose, deep-set eyes, and high cheekbones. A thick black mustache covered his upper lip. His mouth was set yet traced with a slight smile.

"Buenas tardes, Señorita. Señor." The officer spoke with a deep, velvet voice.

"Señor Commandante." Breed nodded.

"Captain Epidio Morales, a sus ordenes."

"Señor Morales, I'm James Stalwart. This is Miss Prentice."

"Mucho gusto, Señorita Prentice." He tipped his sombrero.

"What brings you to our country, Señor Stalwart?"

"Business, which is now finished. We are heading back north."

"Bueno, pero hace calor. It is not smart to travel at this time of day," the officer cautioned them.

"Well, yes. We know. But we're anxious to return." Breed bit his tongue for the choice of words.

"You like our country, Señorita Prentice?"

"Uh, yes, I do." Josie was startled the officer bothered to ask her a question. "But as, you said, it's too hot."

"Are you in the same business as Señor Stalwart?"

"Ah, yes . . . I'm . . ." Josie groped for words.

Breed cut her off. "No, she's not." Breed was uncomfortable with the contradiction.

"Exactly what is your business, Señor Stalwart?"

"When not working for the U.S. Army, I'm a trader."

Breed's mind raced, trying to anticipate the next question and extricate himself at the same time.

"How can you leave your Army job?" Captain Morales was puzzled.

"I'm on special leave." Breed stretched the truth.

"*Que bueno*. Were you on Army business or other business in the town of Dos Diablos?"

"A little of both," was Breed's clumsy reply.

Satisfied at the moment, Captain Morales turned to Lieutenant Del Rio and ordered him, in Spanish, into Dos Diablos to insure everything was in order. The junior officer mustered five men and rode for the pueblo. Breed turned to Josie and quietly explained what had happened.

"We're in trouble now. Those six are headed for the pueblo."

"Why can't you just tell him the truth?"

"He wouldn't believe it. Would you?"

"I see what you mean," was Josie's defeated reply.

The captain addressed Breed. "Your business went well, I hope?"

"Yes, very well." Breed flinched inside. Killed three men in his town and you tell him it went well.

"Where is your Indian from, Señor Stalwart."

"He's a Mescalero. I don't know his past."

"His name, *por favor.*"

"No-Feet," Breed replied.

"No-Feet?" The captain questioned. "But he has feet, no?"

Breed laughed at the question. He tried to explain. "It's a joke, a nickname." The captain didn't understand. *Es un chiste,* Breed offered. As soon as the words left his mouth, Breed realized the seriousness of the slip of tongue. At the same time Captain Morales recognized his error in speaking so openly to the lieutenant while in front of Breed.

"My men will return shortly, as you know. I trust everything will be satisfactory." The officer paused to measure Breed. And perhaps to give him one final chance to level with him. "What were you trading, Señor Stalwart?" It was more an order than a question.

"I traded several pistols. They're in my saddlebag. Let me show you."

Breed untied the flap and gingerly pulled a pistol out by the barrel. He handed it to the captain butt first.

"Surely you have more, no?" Morales sought more information.

"Yes, Captain Morales. I have two more. If you would like I'll get them." Breed tried to cover the oversight.

The captain closely examined the .45 after unloading it. He tested the trigger pull and cylinder movement. The cylinder was tight and he spun it several times with satisfaction. "This is a fine pistol, Señor Stalwart. I especially like the bone handles." The captain fondly held the pistol. Suddenly he changed the direction of the conversation. "May I speak with your Indian for a moment?"

"No-Feet, come here," Breed called the Apache.

The captain spoke with the Apache in the local dialect, much to the surprise of Breed and No-Feet. The Indian grunted replies and gave no more information than was absolutely necessary. No-Feet realized his answers would determine to a substantial degree whether they stayed here forever or rode across the border.

Time moved with the sun. The lieutenant returned from the pueblo of Dos Diablos. The captain distanced himself from Breed as he talked with the junior officer. As the conversation continued, the lieutenant countered Captain Morales. The captain spoke sharply, ending all arguments. As he approached, Breed stepped forward to meet him.

"Captain Morales, as a gesture of friendship, I would like to give you the bone-handled pistol."

The officer was pleased, and thanked Breed for the pistol. He then confronted Breed. "Señor Stalwart, we have a problem. A most serious one." The officer was grave.

"What might that be, Captain?" Breed knew what was coming.

"Three dead men in Dos Diablos. You know anything about them, Señor Stalwart?"

Breed motioned to the officer. "Please, Captain. May we talk?" Breed sat in the shade of his horse, the captain squatted nearby.

Twenty minutes later the officer stood and approached his men. He spoke and several broke away to rummage through their saddlebags. Moments later the captain returned with a short-handled shovel and a skillet. "Señor Stalwart, please dig three graves. With your friend's help, of course." He nodded at No-Feet.

"Mark the spot, Captain."

The officer stepped forward, etched a deep X with

the heel of his boot, then made two more beside his original mark.

Breed and No-Feet began to dig. Breed unbuttoned his shirt and rolled up his sleeves. No-Feet's leather vest was sweat-soaked; beads of sweat trickled down his face. The Mexicans clustered around the grave sites and talked, napped, or cleaned their rifles. Josie watched as Breed and No-Feet slowly disappeared into their respective graves. When Captain Morales indicated the graves were deep enough, Breed and No-Feet began to work together on the third hole. The loose sand made the job twice as difficult. With the task nearly completed, Captain Morales strode to the grave and spoke.

"Excellent work. My compliments. Your one chance to dig graves and you do well." The captain's insinuation that this was their final act poleaxed Breed. "Out of the hole," Morales ordered. "You will stand in front of the graves." Josie came and stood beside Breed.

Captain Morales barked orders to his men. *"Muchachos, adelante, rapido."* Six soldiers fell into place fifteen feet behind Breed, Josie, and No-Feet. Three men knelt, the other three stood behind them in a tight group. Breed felt this a pitiful end to his life, executed in some no-named part of Mexico.

"Turn and face the firing squad," ordered Captain Morales. The trio had their backs to the graves.

Breed heard a horse's footstep in the soft sand as it approached from the rear. He glanced out of the corner of his eye and saw three *Federales* ride to the graves. Each horse had a body draped over its rump. Josie sneaked a peek. Breed heard her sigh of relief. Three bodies were unceremoniously dumped into the graves. Breed looked at Josie. Tears streaked her dirty face.

"Teniente Del Rio," Captain Morales called.

The lieutenant stepped forward and stationed himself beside the squad.

"Listos," he ordered. Six rifles came to port arms.

"Apunten." The rifles were shouldered.

"Disparen." Six rifles fired as one in a thunderous clap.

Breed staggered a step back. Josie's knees buckled. No-Feet flinched. All three had closed their eyes. The rebound of the volley across the desert told them they were alive. Breed slowly sank to the ground beside Josie and put his arm around her. She buried her face in her hands and quietly wept.

Captain Morales dismissed the detail. He walked to Breed, offered his hand, and pulled him to his feet. "Finish your task here, Señor Stalwart. You are then free to go. I do have a word of advice. Don't do any more business down here. *Comprende?*"

"I understand, Captain Morales. You have my word."

The Mexicans mounted and rode away from the graves. Captain Morales turned in his saddle and spoke to Breed. "Señor Stalwart, I want to thank you for a favor. Well, actually three favors. I have waited long to catch those three *cabrones*. Border problems, politics, as you know. You answered my prayers. *Muchisimas gracias.*" Breed saluted the officer. Captain Morales touched the brim of his hat.

Josie had questions she wanted answered. The one foremost in her mind was why the Mexican had shot the volley over the dead men.

Breed laughed at the question, then reflected on the serious side of it. "How many people do you think heard that volley?" Josie shrugged, not having any idea. "I would venture a guess, several dozen. The message is loud and clear. You get caught by the *Federales,* that's the last sound on earth you'll ever hear. It's quite effective."

CHAPTER
11

Fort Manning was a tempest of activity. General Clemments had completed his tour of duty in the southwest and was back in command of the fort. Colonel Prentice, relieved of his command and duties, was in limbo pending the official results of the military investigation. These inquiries encompassed the missing rifles, the kidnapping of Miss Prentice, the murder of Corporal Calhoun, and the desertion of Sergeant Stalwart. The judge advocate's office had supplied twice the necessary manpower. Every aspect of the four special investigations was checked, then double-checked, with no progress made.

Colonel Prentice could add nothing of value to the growing indictment of facts against him. The colonel had not taken a sober breath since Josie's disappearance. But General Clemments put an abrupt end to that upon his return. The junior officer could recall nothing concerning the night Josie vanished.

First Sergeant Fitz's run of luck continued with the military sleuths. Fitz had generously volunteered his services on two search parties that scoured the land for a trace of Miss Prentice. Both searches failed to turn up a clue of the young lady.

Fitz was confident he had left no loose ends. Colonel Prentice had been successfully silenced. The officer was not to be believed in his liquored condition. Corporal Calhoun, his sole accomplice, was deposited six feet under. Miss Prentice was Lacy's property and headache and would remain so until he tired of her, then he would trade her to the Mexicans. With Irish luck, Breed would be on the run for life, dodging bounty hunters and lawmen. Fitz thought of his fat bank account in Deliverance, the neighboring town, and relaxed. He dreamed about the endless opportunities that awaited him: cattle buyer, landowner, or gambler. "Hell, I could gamble 'til I drop and have money left over," he confided.

With this newfound feeling of confidence, First Sergeant Fitz set about his daily chores with the express intention of drawing no attention to himself. People commented he was acting unusually pleasant, almost human. The last investigation concerning the rifles had been a cakewalk. Fitz's thoughts turned toward retirement from the military and this godawful place. "First Sergeant Shamus Fitzpatrick, U.S. Army, Retired. That warms the heart of an old, cold-hearted sergeant." He laughed at his own humor.

Fitz thought with contempt about Colonel Prentice. Any officer worth his brass would have called Fitz's bluff years ago, but Colonel Prentice wasn't just any other officer. Vanity and ego had come before career. Fitz had played these against the officer like a cudgel of doom. Fitz wondered if he should destroy his half of the aging Civil War orders. No, I'll hold on to them for future use. Upon returning to his quarters, Fitz checked and made sure the paper was wedged securely behind his dresser drawer.

Breed and No-Feet worked feverishly to fill the graves. They wanted to distance themselves from the *Federales* as quickly as possible. Breed realized how fortunate they had been. Josie stood nearby, still visibily shaken. The Mexican soldiers rode casually away, and occasionally glanced in their direction to check on the progress of their task.

"Josie, fetch our horses here." Breed snapped Josie out of her daze. "The soldiers left them near the draw." He pointed the shovel in the direction.

She hurried off, needing no spurring. While not a stranger to frontier life, the lessons Josie had learned in the last few days taught her more than she had thought possible about survival. She was terrified of men like Lacy and the Willittses. How could they live, fight, and die with such casual fatalistic acceptance? She understood and appreciated the confident nature of Captain Morales. He held the power of life and death in his judgments. Good fortune had been with them in this situation. She remembered how Breed had struggled with Captain Morales's mind game, somehow talking his way out of a dicey predicament.

As she walked the horses, Breed and No-Feet met her. They were anxious to ride, and mounted quickly. None of them looked at the graves as they trotted past. Breed glanced back at the Mexicans and Captain Morales. Breed nodded his head. "Thank you, Captain." The officer returned the nod. "That we don't meet again, Señor Stalwart."

With No-Feet out front, Breed and Josie followed and headed for the beckoning mountains. It was late afternoon; lengthening shadows and softening sunlight touched the desert in soft pastels. They skirted the pueblo of Agua Dulce and found a campsite. Fort Manning was a hard four hours' ride. Tomorrow would come soon enough.

A small glowing mesquite fire warmed the three. A sheltered creek bed embraced them for the night. The rabbits No-Feet had killed were simmering over the coals. Josie had been squeamish about eating something she had seen alive moments before. The tasty smell quickly changed her mind. Her stomach was not to be denied. No-Feet produced his cup, coffee, and sugar. They shared the thick brew. After dinner the Apache disappeared into the night. He was apprehensive knowing word of the triple killing was out. Campesino would avenge the death of his gun-runners.

"Josie, I have to ask you a question." Breed was

uncertain how to broach the delicate subject. "When you were with Lacy, did he . . ." Breed searched for words. "Was he able . . ." He could not go beyond that point.

"For heaven sakes, Breed." Josie was slightly amused at his awkward approach. "What are you asking?"

"Well, did he, you know what I mean . . . ?"

"Did he violate me?" she asked straight out, then laughed. "No, he didn't feel up to it." A smile creased her full lips. "The intentions were there but he was too sore. He held off those awful cousins at gunpoint."

Breed laughed with relief. He was amused by Josie's feisty and rebellious attitude.

"You aren't concerned about my well-being, now, are you?" she jokingly asked.

"As a matter of fact I am." He heated up under the collar as she touched on inner feelings.

Josie realized her mistake and replied with sincerity, "I thank you for your concern. I appreciate it."

"You're welcome," was the terse reply.

Silence settled heavily between them. Neither was good at small talk. "Breed," Josie broke the silence. "I have something to show you. I don't understand it, maybe you will."

She turned away from him and reached inside her bodice for the torn slip of paper she had removed from her father's clinched fist. As she handed it to Breed, her spirits soared. "What does it mean?"

Breed studied it closely, reread it several times

before answering. "Orders. Without the other half it's meaningless."

Her hopes dashed, Josie burst into tears. She had counted too much on the paper. Breed was startled at her outburst and reached to comfort her.

"Hold on now," he pleaded with her. "We'll find out what's behind it. Don't worry." He pulled her closer to him. "No more tears, please."

She looked at him, her faith partially restored. "No more tears, I promise." She sniffed, then spoke. "You'll help me?"

"My word on it. When we return to Fort Manning tomorrow, we'll go straight to your father and show him the note. We'll confront Fitz also and get to the bottom of this."

They talked for a while, both feeling more comfortable with the other. Breed occasionally put pieces of mesquite onto the glowing coals. The warmth of the desert had gone with the sun. The night had a chill. The sky was inky black, dotted with countless diamonds of sparkling light.

"I'm beat. Gun-trading tuckered me out," Breed said with a smile.

"I didn't realize the business was so exhausting."

"It has its moments, doesn't it?"

Josie was taken aback with Breed's words. After a shootout that left three men dead, and walking a tightrope with the *Federales,* that was all he had to say.

Breed spread his bedroll. There was one blanket.

"Where do I sleep?"

"You have two choices. Next to me or with No-Feet." Josie's temper flared visibly. "Now, don't jump before you're spurred," Breed cautioned her. "I'll give you the side by the fire, you'll stay warmer. If you wake during the night, put more mesquite on the embers."

"Promise you'll keep your hands to yourself?" she questioned him.

"Uh huh," he answered with a grin. "You promise you'll keep your hands to yourself also?" he demanded in return.

"Of course," she bristled at the insinuation.

Breed didn't catch a wink of sleep. He was troubled by thoughts of Campesino. With that bandit on the prowl, no one was safe. As he turned, he felt something brush against him. He sat bolt upright and swept his chest clean and roughly knocked Josie's hand away.

"Oh, it's you," he breathed a sigh. "I thought it was a tarantula or a scorpion snuggling up for warmth."

"I'm cold," Josie shivered. "I just wanted to get warm."

Once they settled down, Breed pulled the blanket around them. Again he felt her hands. "What about your promise to keep hands off?" he confronted her.

Josie rose onto her elbow. Her face, tinted a light orange from the small fire, had a devilish grin on it. "I never was good at keeping my word," she replied.

Following a hasty breakfast of cold rabbit and tepid coffee, the three broke camp and rode north. Dawn cracked the black night with a silver streak on the horizon. The mountains that had loomed closely last

evening appeared to be miles away, their rugged out-
lines crisply silhouetted in the predawn light. Somewhere between here and the mountains Campesino
would find them. Breed rode beside Josie. "If something happens, ride like there'll be no tomorrow. If we
get caught, there might not be one." His tone added
weight to his words.

"Do you think Campesino will find us?" She
searched his face for reassurance. She didn't find it.

"Gal, you best pray he doesn't. Campesino makes
Lacy and the Willittses look like church deacons. I'll
tell you one thing, they will have a fight on their hands
before they get us." He winked at her. She felt better.

Josie shuddered at the thought of capture. Lacy and
the Willitts brothers were revolting. The possibility of
someone worse petrified her.

No-Feet was a short distance ahead, diligently
searching for signs. His rifle was cradled across his lap
ready for use. He stopped short of a bluff that overlooked two converging arroyos. The Apache looked at
hoofprints in the sand. Breed rode up beside him.
"Those tracks are fresh. Maybe a dozen horses," No-
Feet spoke as he searched for the riders.

"Are they from the Mexican soldiers?" Josie asked
Breed.

"No. They seldom ride this far north. This country
belongs to the strongest and cruelest. Campesino.
What do you think, No-Feet?"

"Go there." He pointed to the left arroyo. "Away
from the others."

"Ride! Remember, gal, if we get caught, even the Lord can't help us." Breed's look told it all.

They fell off the bluff prodding their hesitant mounts. The animals hunkered on their haunches as the bank crumbled beneath them. After the dust settled, they headed for a narrow side arroyo. No-Feet crossed the open ground like a ghost, Josie right behind. Breed was three quarters of the way across when a shout broke the early morning calm.

"Go," Breed hollered as he dug hard into the mare. "Get the hell out of here."

No-Feet had heard the shout and was riding at a full gallop. Josie's mare lagged and Breed rode alongside. He savagely whipped the horse across the rump. They thundered out of the arroyo side by side onto the rolling desert. Breed could hear the Mexicans ride out behind them.

"Push 'er hard, Josie," Breed yelled excitedly. "We've got to open up more distance."

No-Feet's pony set a punishing pace. Josie worked her mare hard to keep up. Breed's mare seemed to enjoy the challenge. The Mexicans were content to hold back, and made no attempt to close the distance.

A scanning glance off to the right electrified Breed. Half a dozen riders paralleled them and matched their pace. The front rider was unmistakably Campesino. He looked like a plug of mahogany glued to his horse as he rode effortlessly. His black mustache accented a smirk that twisted his mouth. Breed watched him closely, regarding him as a dangerous foe. Campesino and his men rode the hillock that merged gently into the desert. Whoever reached the open desert first would live.

Breed and No-Feet were thinking alike. The Apache shifted his rifle to shoot left-handed. Breed did the same with his .45–70. He didn't shoot well left-handed, but he had no choice. Campesino made a sweeping gesture for his men to fan out from the ridge. No-Feet carefully sighted on the second man and shot. The Mexican was knocked over the rump of his horse. His body ricocheted twice off the hard-packed desert and tumbled to stop against the prickly spines of a cactus. No-Feet never ceased to amaze Breed with his riding and shooting abilities. The Apache was part of his pony; together they flowed in fluid motion. Breed leaned forward, partially stood in the stirrups, and shot at Campesino. Breed knew immediately he was off the mark.

Campesino responded by raising his new Winchester and drawing down solidly on Breed. A momentary chilling death feeling churned through Breed as he watched the bandit take aim. Breed leaned forward along the neck of his mare. The next seconds were frozen in slow motion. Breed stared as Campesino gently pulled the trigger. The puff of smoke meant death. Breed tensed and braced for the killing bullet. Campesino's rifle disintegrated in his hands. Jagged pieces of steel smashed through his skull. The Mexican *jefe* never knew what killed him. As Campesino tumbled off his mount, his leather leggings caught in the stirrup. Campesino's body bounced off the ground and panicked his horse. The terrified animal smelled blood and stampeded wildly across the desert, dragging the dead Mexican behind.

The wicked buss of a bullet snapped Breed back to the chase. Both groups rapidly converged on the flats. Breed realized he hadn't reloaded, and quickly did so. A bearded Mexican aimed and shot at Breed. No smoke from the rifle. No sound of the shot. Nothing. The man ejected the spent brass and levered in a new round. He shot a second time at Breed. The rifle barrel exploded. Razor-sharp pieces of shrapnel flew in all directions. The man grabbed his throat, as a tick-sized shard had severed his jugular vein. The Mexican stared at his bloody hands and shirt as his life spilled away. With a casual grace he slumped and fell from his galloping horse.

The last rider, "buck neked" except for a loincloth, shot at Josie. No bullet came from his rifle. He continued to ride, and carefully ejected the shell. The bullet was still in the brass. The Indian threw it aside in disgust and levered in a new round. He shot a second time at Josie. Nothing happened. Breed swerved closer toward the Indian and shouldered his .45–70. Breed centered the bead on the Indian's side and quickly shot. The five-hundred-grain bullet swept the Indian off his horse like a dust devil sweeping a tumbleweed off the desert.

After watching their leader and three of their number drop, the remaining flank riders quit the chase. The riders that followed Breed out of the arroyo also abandoned pursuit. As a final defiant jesture, the Mexicans fired a volley at the three rapidly disappearing riders. The resulting barrel and breech explosions wounded two Mexicans and killed one.

Gunnery First Sergeant Stan Alcorn had done his job well. Immediately after the arrival of the second rifle shipment at Fort Manning, he had requisitioned them under the pretext of a final inspection. With the rifles safe in the gunnery shop, Alcorn carried out his end of the deal for Breed. Not only were the rifles "serviced" but some ammunition was "inspected" also. The gunner had filed some of the firing pins enough so they would fail under the adrenaline rush of battle. A half-dozen trigger main springs were similarly weakened. Gunner Alcorn knew from experience that rifles were roughly treated under fire, with no consideration given to careful handling.

Gunner, counting on this predictable behavior, doctored the shells. He hoped no one would notice the full loads didn't sound when shaken. The resulting pressures from these loads far exceeded the design of both breech and barrel. A handful of shells were salt-and-pepper loads, with just enough sawdust to give them weight. The "blackbeard" Mexican who'd shot at Breed had only a hint of powder in the first shell. It had lodged in the barrel. The second shell was a full load. The resulting explosion was a fatal one for him. The "bare-assed" Indian who'd shot twice at Josie had two sawdust loads. Neither shell had had enough gunpowder to separate the bullet from the brass.

By midday Breed, Josie, and No-Feet were in the pine-covered foothills of the Arizona Territory. The air was cool and clean. The mountains of Mexico were shimmering and dancing in the distance. The blast-furnace air and blistering heat of Mexico were behind them. "Let's stop and water at the logjam," Breed suggested to Josie. "We'll ride directly to the fort from there."

"Do you dare go back?"

"I have to," he flatly stated. "Besides, I'm not guilty of anything." He laughed. "Well, maybe stupidity. I'll need your help."

"Breed, you know I'll stand up for you. We've got to get Fitz. He's behind this and the evil that torments Daddy." A renewed sense of purpose boosted Josie. She would fight to save her father.

Breed met Josie's eyes and winked at her. She smiled back at him. The ride into the thick timber of the logjam passed quickly. At the spring they indulged themselves in the cold, teeth-chilling water.

CHAPTER
12

"No one move down there!" the voice boomed from the trees that surrounded the logjam. No-Feet and Breed had been careless and let their guard down because they were close to Fort Manning.

"Unbuckle your gun belts and let them fall. Put your rifles down. *Slowly!*" The orders were barked at them. "Now, belly down on the ground and put your hands out to the sides."

Breed did as he was ordered, knelt slowly, then lay down. No-Feet defiantly stood. He wouldn't lie down for any man, let alone a white man.

"You blink and you're a dead Indian," the unseen voice hollered again. No-Feet stood motionless. Breed searched the thick timber but saw no one. "Miss Prentice, would you please step away from both men?"

Two soldiers materialized out of the thick jack oak and cautiously approached. Three others stood to reveal their concealed positions as they covered their fellow troopers. The closest soldier knelt beside Breed and quickly tied his hands behind his back. No-Feet received the same reward. Breed was roughly hauled to his feet and saw the remaining soldiers come forward. Lieutenant Pillings, junior cavalry officer, stepped out of the underbrush and addressed Breed. "Mister Stalwart, it is my duty to escort you to Fort Manning. The orders read 'Dead or Alive.' I trust you will choose the latter." He smiled, but let Breed know he intended to take him in one way or the other.

"Sir, the sooner I get back the better." Breed was anxious to return. "I'm ready when you are." He realized he had no say-so in the matter.

"Are you all right, Miss Prentice?" The officer was concerned about her well-being.

"Yes, Lieutenant. I'm fine, thank you."

"Good. Your father will be pleased to see you." The officer turned to his men. "Kelly, Lockwood, fetch our horses. We'll ride immediately."

As the ten soldiers and their charges rode across the field, a soft breeze rustled the mid-thigh grass, making the riders appear to be floating on green waves. The heavy, timber gates of Fort Manning were opened by four soldiers. Half a dozen armed troopers provided cover. After the last rider passed through the gate, it was closed and barred. General Clemments, flanked on either side by a covey of staff officers, waited patiently as the detail rode directly for his office. Lieutenant Pillings halted in front of the general and saluted.

"Sir, I'm pleased to deliver Miss Prentice. Unharmed, I might add." He smiled with relief. "Mister Stalwart and his scout are returned without incident, sir."

"Well done, Lieutenant," the general replied as he returned the salute. "Dismiss your detail and stand down until further notice."

The general stepped off the porch and walked to Josie's horse. He helped her dismount. "Miss Prentice, are you well? Is there anything I can do?"

"Thank you, General." She brushed hair away from her face. "I beg an urgent favor."

"Name it," he replied forcefully. "If I can do it, I will."

"General Clemment, the man entirely responsible for this sordid affair is First Sergeant Fitz. He should be brought here and made to answer for his actions."

The general remained by her side, puzzled by the abrupt and unusual request.

"General, please." She clutched his arm, her desperation sincere and convincing. "Sergeant Stalwart is innocent and First Sergeant Fitz is culpable."

"One moment, Lieutenant Pillings," the general shouted to the departing officer. "Take a three-man detail and bring First Sergeant Fitz to my quarters immediately." The lieutenant saluted, turned away, and chose his men. "Lieutenant," the general added, "if you have to drag the first sergeant screaming and kicking, do so. Also secure his quarters. I want everything of value under guard."

Breed and No-Feet were hauled off their horses, and stood nearby. "Corporal, untie those men," the general ordered as he ushered Josie up the stairs. "I want to see them in my office immediately."

"But, sir, you'll need guards." The young soldier was concerned with the general's safety.

"Corporal," declared the commanding officer, "I'll assume full responsibility for these three. Now, get with it," he brusquely ordered.

Inside the office, Breed and Josie were seated in front of the general's desk. No-Feet squatted by the door. "Lieutenants Miller and Hotchkiss," the general addressed the officers, "I want you to write down every word spoken from this moment on." The general turned and fixed his eyes on Breed. "Mister Stalwart. From the beginning. Give me the details as best you can remember. Leave nothing out. What you say here will weight heavily on two military careers, Colonel Prentice's and yours." A smile creased his face. "And mine," he added. "Perhaps we can also salvage the reputation and honor of this young lady. Proceed."

Word of Breed's and Josie's return spread through the fort in haste. The veteran Indian fighters were delighted. Many had wagered Breed would return and beat the trumped-up charges. The younger men knew a good soldier had returned. Friends of the Prentices were relieved with Josie's safe return. They prayed her presence would bring the colonel out of his depression and put life back into him. Since the night of Josie's disappearance, the colonel had withdrawn from the outside world. He would have drunk himself to death if it had not been for Sawbones and Hattie, the general's wife. They worked together to sober the colonel up, and force-fed him to keep him alive. The colonel was moved to a private corner of the infirmary where he was under twenty-four-hour supervision. His physical problems were under control but his state of mind was unreachable.

First Sergeant Fitz was struck dumb, and refused to believe his eyes as he watched Breed and Josie escorted into the fort. He stepped into the shadows of the stables and stumbled into a beam. Using it for support, he realized his intricate plots had gone straight to hell. There would be no way he could bluff his way out of this. Fitz knew his tenure at Fort Manning and in the U.S. Army had been abruptly terminated.

"Damn it," he swore softly. "This's a little sudden. I still had plans for Colonel Prentice. Well"—he shrugged—"it was not to be."

Fitz needed his gear and papers. He especially wanted the other half of those orders that had served him so well. If he could wait 'til dark, his chances would improve considerably. Fitz cursed himself for letting Calhoun talk him into getting separate keys for their strongbox in the Bank of Deliverance. He remembered seeing the key attached to a pocketknife the night Calhoun's partnership was terminated in the stockade. The sarge searched every possible hiding place trying to locate it. No luck. He even considered digging Calhoun's body up to find it. With General Clemments's return, tighter security precautions were enforced. Guard details were beefed up. No one left the fort without a written chit from the old man.

The sunset colors were a splash of vivid golden yellows and flaming oranges. Fitz sneaked to the corner of his quarters. He heard voices from within and pressed closer to the window.

"Dawson, Kelly," Lieutenant Pillings instructed, "you two have the watch until 2400. These quarters are secured by orders of General Clemments. No one enters this room," he emphasized to the young soldiers. "If either of you see the first sergeant, sound the alarm and arrest him on sight. Understood?"

"Yes, sir," they answered in unison.

"Now, get something to eat before you relieve Smith and Holden. Be back soon so they can eat." The two soldiers left the room and headed for the dining hall.

"Sir," Private Holden asked, "is there anything of importance left in here? The room has been torn apart."

"No," was the officer's quick reply. "All the papers, letters, everything is in the general's office. There is nothing left here but you two."

Fitz stepped into the dark shadows as the officer passed by. The first sarge had lost his trump card with Colonel Prentice. "Not to worry," he spoke quietly to himself. "Well, good-bye, Colonel Prentice. Thank you very much." He smiled, turned, and disappeared into the fading light.

It was 2100 and Breed was hoarse from talking. Breed, Josie, and the general had taken a dinner break, and walked off the fatigue from being sequestered in the stifling office. Breed's deposition continued after their return. The general's staff had a stack of papers and writer's cramp.

"I'm finished, sir. You know the rest." Breed breathed a sigh of relief. "We were brought directly to you."

"In reference to your involvement, Miss Prentice, are these the facts as best you can recall?"

"Yes, General. They're correct."

"Excellent. Lieutenant Miller," the general requested of his two officers, "requisition whatever manpower you need to formalize these notes by tomorrow afternoon. If you can have them done earlier, fine."

The officer nodded numbly. The request meant at

least twelve hours of work. The lieutenant stood, saluted, and left the room.

"There are two other matters to discuss with the both of you. I realize it's late and you need rest. These matters are of immediate importance." The general addressed them as he took a large envelope from his desk drawer.

General Clemments handed Breed an Official Mail envelope. The flap was secured with a wax seal. Breed broke the seal and read the enclosed letter.

FROM: Office of Judge Advocate, Major General Buell C. M. McDonald.
Fifth Judicial District
Prescott, Department of Arizona

TO:
General Shenandoah Clemments III
Fifth United States Army, Commander
Fort Manning, Department of Arizona.

General Clemments:

In reference to the case of Stalwart, James vs The United States Army, case #344-19-JRP, I respectfully submit that following an exhaustive and comprehensive review by Captain Morris and the Judicial Review Board, Fifth Judicial District, I am legally obligated to overturn the majority decision on the aforementioned case #344-19-JRP. This dismissal is based upon the following misapplications of the judicial process.

(1). Improper judicial procedure regarding the omission and subsequent violation of the defendant's right to a fair and impartial hearing.

(2). Biased and prejudicial board.

(3). Conflicting testimony and questions of credibility of principal prosecution witness.

In summation, while the review board neither supports nor condones the action of the aforementioned defendant (Stalwart, James, case #344-19-JRP), the board finds the constitutional and judicial rights as mandated by the Articles of War were improperly executed and the defendant inadequately represented. Upon recommendation from both the counsel for the defense and the review board, the military court-martial selection process will be carefully reviewed and the board members upgraded. It is paramount the judicial system be staffed with top-notch officers. Our judicial obligations are our first priority.

As of this date, all charges, sentences, demotions, and loss of privileges will be dropped against the defendant. All rank and pay will herewith be fully reinstated to the defendant, James Stalwart.

Sergeant James Stalwart was deprived of evaluation and promotion during this court-martial hearing. It is the board's recommendation, with your approval, that Sergeant Stalwart be granted a promotion in rank to First Sergeant.

By order of,
Major General Buell C. M. McDonald
First United States Army, Commander

Breed reread the last paragraph. He was incredulous. A fleeing murderer, kidnapper, and gun-runner this morning. Now totally exonerated with the stroke of a pen this afternoon. "General, does this mean . . . ?"

"Yes, First Sergeant, it does, and exactly as stated." The general walked to his liquor cabinet and retrieved a bottle of brandy and glasses. He did the honor and passed the glasses to Breed and Josie. "I propose a toast." He raised his glass to Breed. "To First Sergeant Stalwart. My next scout on the southern campaigns. A pleasure to have you in my company." They sipped their brandy and reveled in the good news. "I will tell you something I trust will not leave this room. I neither liked nor trusted Fitz since the day I met the man." The general smiled at his revelation. "I take this opportunity to commend your judgment at Twin Buttes. It must have been a terrible choice." The general looked at Breed with compassion. "As a result of this farce of a court-martial maybe we'll get soldiers on the review with some backbone. We need men who understand this war and appreciate the circumstances."

"Thank you, sir." Breed was still dazed by the turn of events.

" 'Nuff said," the general interrupted him. "Dismiss yourself and turn in. The damned paperwork can wait 'til tomorrow."

Breed stood and snapped a crisp salute to General Clemments. "Evening, sir."

"Evening, First Sergeant," was the general's heartfelt reply. A sharp salute followed his words. Breed excused himself, walked past Josie, and smiled at her. She gave his arm a tender squeeze in return.

After Breed left, the general refilled his glass. He sat in his battered chair and contemplated his next move. The next several minutes were uncomfortably quiet. General Clemments leaned forward, grabbed his drink, and knocked back the shot. As the brandy simmered its way down his throat he faced Josie.

"Please forgive me, Josie, for keeping you this long but serious charges have been filed against your father." The general paused as if to rekindle his strength. "Young lady, I've known you since you were a tadpole and your father for well nigh twenty years. I left this fort in his capable hands and return to find the damnedest shambles and your father drunk on his ear." The general grasped her hand. "Please tell me what ill-omened luck has befallen this man? And his responsibilities?"

Josie was touched by the general's impassioned plea. "General Clemments, I have no answers." She sadly hung her head. "I can't reach my father. He withdraws into his drunken shell and shuts me completely out."

"There has to be something." He searched her face. "Is there any one person who sets him off? Perhaps remembering your mother? Bless her gracious soul," he added with reverence.

"Ah, General, there is something. Why didn't I think of it." She slapped her hands together out of frustration. Josie turned her back to the general and pulled the torn piece of paper from her dress. "I found this with

Daddy on one of his drinking nights. It seems to involve Sergeant Fitz in some way. He has some strange hold over my father."

As she spoke she handed the paper to the general. He glanced at it, went to his cabinet, and returned with the other half of the paper. He fitted the two pieces together and read the completed message for the first time.

Captain Prentice;
Where in the hell are your troops. We're waiting for your reinforcements. It is imperative that you join my command. My counter thrust depends upon your presence. Report to me immediately.
Brig. Gen. Sam Zook

"Orders from General Zook to your father during the battle of Fredericksburg. I know Sam Zook. Hell of a good soldier," the general commented forcefully. "Excuse me for a minute while I dig into this matter. *Wilson!*" the general shouted. The general's voice no sooner died than his aide hurried into the office.

"Sir?" he asked in pained anticipation.

"Find Lieutenant Pillings. I want to know exactly where he found this half note." The general waved the paper in front of his aide. "Give me the answer in five minutes. Now git."

"Yes, sir," the man replied with resignation. Yet he was in motion, halfway out the door when he answered.

"Josie, I don't understand why Sergeant Fitz had half

of this message." He looked at her for an answer. "Where did you get your half?"

Josie told him of finding her father passed out after seeing Fitz and of taking the paper from her father's clinched fist. "I still don't know why it upsets him so. He gets blind drunk and won't talk to anyone."

"My dear, I think it's time we find out." The general stood, snagged his Stetson off the brass hall tree, and offered his arm to Josie.

As the general opened the door he was nearly flattened by Wilson. The aide was out of breath and couldn't speak for several seconds.

"Well, Lieutenant. What did you learn?" the general impatiently prodded him.

"Lieutenant Pillings said he found the paper stuck to the back of the bottom drawer of Fitz's dresser." The aide gasped out his reply.

"Good work, son." The general beamed. "I'll be in the infirmary if I'm needed. Dismissed." He saluted the aide. "Come along, Josie." The general walked briskly toward the infirmary with Josie in tow.

Despite the dirt and grit, Sawbones kept a spotless infirmary. His was a thankless job, but nevertheless the sheets were white, towels clean, and his instruments of "fixin' and healin'" sterile. The cramped room was orderly yet cramped with six cots. Sawbones worked at his battered rolltop desk doing battle against government paperwork. His mood reflected his loathing of it.

"Evening, Doc," called General Clemments as he ushered Josie into the room.

"In a damned pig's eye it is," he grumbled, then turned around to greet the general. "Oh, 'scuse me, Miss Prentice." He rose to greet Josie. "I'm delighted at your safe return, but I thought you would keep better company." He smiled slyly at her.

"The hell you say," retorted the general.

"Please, gentlemen," Josie feigned her best southern drawl, "I've nevah heard such *crude* language in mah entirah life." She couldn't keep a straight face.

They laughed together. Giving each other sass was an ingrained ritual.

"How's the colonel?" the general inquired. "We would like to see him if he's feeling fit."

"General, physically the man is sound enough," Sawbones complained. "What I'm unable to heal is the hurting inside. He turns me off as if I weren't there," the doc stated dejectedly. "Maybe when he sees your lovely face, Josie, it will bring him back. I certainly hope so."

Sawbones escorted Josie to the partitioned corner of the infirmary. The doc pulled aside the curtain and let her enter. Josie sat on the edge of the cot. Colonel Prentice slept fitfully and tossed about. In the soft lanternlight Josie gasped when she saw her father's ashen, sunken face. Had she not known him so well, she would have had difficulty recognizing him. Josie mustered her strength and shook him gently.

"Daddy, it's me, Josie. I've come back and I'm all right."

She repeated her words three times before they

seemed to sink in. Her father struggled and shook his head as if trying to clear it. Suddenly he lurched upright. "My child, my God," he cried out. "It's really you."

He fought his tangled nightshirt, hugged Josie tightly, and wept softly. The exhausted colonel buried his face in the hollow of his daughter's shoulder in embarrassment at his weakness and open display of emotion. The general and Sawbones discreetly walked to the doc's desk. Josie comforted her father until he regained his composure. The colonel gently pushed Josie away and gazed at her intently.

"It's you," he said in disbelief. "Really you. Surely you must know what great joy your return brings to me. To see you again makes me want to live." The colonel exuded contentment. Life seemed to flow back into his hollow frame as his self-inflicted depression began to lift. A slight blush of color tinted his cheeks.

"Daddy, tell me what happened to you. Do you want to die?" she probed, searching for answers.

"No, dear, you're wrong. It's all right now that you're back," he bluffed. "I'll handle my problems and not bother you with them." His weakness overcame him.

"Daddy, you can't handle them. Look at your condition." Josie lost the fight to curb her tongue. "You're a tired old man and a drunk to boot." Pent-up frustrations spilled out. Her wrath startled her. Colonel Prentice sought to reassure Josie, and clasped her hands. She jerked them free as if burned by his touch. "Daddy,

I won't put up with your falsehoods. What does Sergeant Fitz hold over you? *What!*" she demanded. "That rogue will be the death of you. Rid yourself of him." Josie looked her father squarely in the eye. She would not back down.

General Clemments and Sawbones overheard the brewing fracas. The general felt the opportunity ripe to confront Colonel Prentice. He stood quietly and soft-shoed to the curtain. The commanding officer parted the curtain, hooked a chair with his toe, and sat. "Neville, the time is now to clear your name." The general firmly addressed the junior officer. "Sergeant Fitz is under arrest at this very moment." General Clemments stretched the truth. "He has leveled serious charges against you. Would you set the record straight?" This appeal was a shabbily disguised order.

A stony silence settled in the sweltering corner of the infirmary. Colonel Prentice glanced at the general, then Josie, and finally at Sawbones. They awaited his response. Off in the distance a coyote yipped at his mate. A thought of a breeze carried the lonely answer. Crickets conversed outside the window.

Colonel Prentice took a deep breath and patted the bed. "Sit here, child. I'll need your support." Josie moved closer to her father's side.

"You've always had it, Daddy." She took his hand.

"General Clemments, Sergeant Fitzpatrick has been blackmailing me since the Battle of Fredericksburg. He has held a threat over me." The colonel spoke forcefully.

General Clemments slipped the torn orders from his pocket. "Do these orders figure in with Sergeant Fitz?" The general leaned forward and handed the paper to Colonel Prentice. The colonel did not look at them. He nodded his head solemnly. "Neville, tell me about the orders. In your own words."

Colonel Prentice, bolstered by the conciliatory gesture, gathered his thoughts. "Sir, I marched with Sumner's Right Grand Division through Fredericksburg. Our objective was to seize Marye's Heights and drive Longstreet off the summit. I left that morning with thirty-two men under my command. After the first assault I had seven men left. Seven!" Colonel Prentice cried out in anguish. "Half of them had never shaved." Colonel Prentice's face was mottled and flushed. "I ordered my men to follow me. We fought to within twenty yards of that stone wall only to be repulsed. I then received those cursed orders from Zook." Colonel Prentice hurled the paper across the room. "Report to my command with your reinforcements. Damn it all to hell. I was the only fit man left. I panicked and ran from that death hill. I crossed the Fredericksburg and Potomac railroad tracks and found shelter in an abandoned warehouse. I left my men. My command." The colonel wept openly.

"How did Sergeant Fitz obtain your orders?" General Clemments gently probed.

"Fitz fought with the Irish Brigade. They too were repulsed from Marye's Heights with heavy losses. Fitz fled the battlefield and sought refuge in the same warehouse. He secretly watched me bury my chevrons. Out of fear of capture I stuffed Zook's orders beneath a floorboard. Fitz presented me with those orders after our battered and beaten Army of the Potomac recrossed the Rappahannock River in defeat. Since that day he has threatened me with exposure if I didn't follow his every whim and fancy."

"My God, man. Why didn't you call his bluff'?" the general asked in disbelief.

"I was too ashamed," Colonel Prentice blurted out. "I had abandoned my men and fled the field of battle in disgrace. My pride and honor was buried beneath the floor of that warehouse." The colonel dropped his face to his chin and hid his face. Before anyone could speak the colonel continued. "A further insult was my field promotion to major for 'bravery and gallantry on the field of battle.' Ha," he exclaimed bitterly, "what a cruel thing is war. I am decorated and promoted by my fellow officers and my men are buried and eulogized." The colonel was silent, and slumped dejectedly. Josie hugged him tightly.

General Clemments slowly stretched the pain from his back and stood. He realized no further information was to be gleaned from Colonel Prentice that evening. As the general parted the curtain, Colonel Prentice called, "Sir, what of my career?"

The general looked at the pathetic figure on the bed. "Neville, I will do what I can but I promise nothing. As an officer it was your duty to fight with your men. And die with them if necessary!" The general stressed his words with a clenched fist. "You let them down and you let the United States Army down, too. I can appreciate the situation of Fredericksburg and Marye's Heights, but soldiers look to their officers for leadership."

General Clemments glared harshly at Colonel Prentice. "I'll attempt to save your pension and support your transfer. I will fight for you as you should have fought for your men."

"Thank you, sir." Neville Prentice felt relief now that he had unburdened his conscience.

Sawbones followed the general out of the infirmary. The night air was crisp, the stars glittered in a clear sky. "What will happen to him, Shenandoah?"

"Doc, I can't say. I know how he felt on the battle field. His only mistakes were in judgment. I can't see shooting a man for stupidity."

"You'd better hope not. There wouldn't be many generals left if you did." Sawbones slipped the insult in.

"You old fart," Clemments retorted. "I'd shoot you but I shan't waste a good bullet. Besides, it probably would bounce off your thick skull. Now leave me be. I've got to extricate my butt from this mess. Night."

The commanding officer of Fort Manning walked the width and breadth of the parade ground lost in thought. The damage to morale and the loss of confidence in the officer corps would take months to mend. "Damn that man," Clemments cursed. "Damn him."

CHAPTER
13

First Sergeant Stalwart returned to full duty the next day at quarters. After assigning men to work details, Breed returned to his quarters and finished his report. He hand-delivered it to General Clemments at eleven o'clock sharp. As Breed walked toward the stables, he palmed Corporal Calhoun's key in his hand, turning it over and over. Its significance eluded him. The night Fitz murdered Calhoun, Breed saw the corporal's knife and key on the desk, and had pocketed both. Breed ambled to the armory to pay First Sergeant Alcorn a courtesy visit. Breed's curiosity over the tampered rifles also needed to be satiated. The gunner was busy at his workbench when Breed entered his shop.

"Hello, Gunner. How the hell you been?" Breed greeted him warmly.

Alcorn stood and met Breed, hand outstretched and grinning like a pig under a gate. "By damn it's good to see you, lad. I knew you'd beat that hollow mockery of a court-martial. Have a seat." Alcorn pointed Breed to one of the stools alongside the workbench. "It does my heart good to know the system still works."

"My friend, without your help, neither Miss Prentice, No-Feet, nor I would be alive today," Breed told him truthfully. "We thank you."

"Ah, hell. Us good guys got to stick together."

Breed flipped the key onto the bench. "What's the

key for, Gunner?" Alcorn side-glanced at the key. "Don't you know nothin'?" He wagged his head in mock disbelief. "It's a strongbox key." He squinted at the tarnished numbers, then commented to Breed, "If I'm not mistaken, it's from the Bank of Deliverance, box 24-C."

Breed felt a tingle of excitement. "How in the hell did you know that?"

"Easy, fool," Alcorn needled him. "The numbers tell it all. First three are the master cast, lot 881. The second set, 04C, is the bank code; I do believe it is Deliverance." Alcorn moved his finger along the line of numbers and letters. "The third set is the box number, 24-C." Alcorn sat back smug and grinnin'. "Us old-timers have more goin' fur us than you young whelps give us credit fur." He smiled slyly. "A pay-master friend of mine explained the system to me years ago. I know for a fact it's the Deliverance bank."

Breed could see the logic in sharing a strongbox with separate keys. With Fitz on the loose it would only be a matter of time before he found a way to get his money.

"Breed, if memory serves me right, you'll need two keys present to open the strongbox. You want a dupli-cate made?"

"That would be great, Gunner. Could you do it by this afternoon?" Breed was reluctant to push him.

"What time?" was the quick answer.

"Around 1500. Now, the real reason for my visit is to ask about those rifles. What did you do to them? The results were nasty, saved me having to shoot several more people," Breed spoofed the gunner.

"I'll bet," gloated the gunner. "I'd a love to seen it. You know how much it hurt me to 'fix' them new rifles. They sure was lovely pieces." Alcorn fondly recalled the new Winchesters, each separately wrapped, and covered with factory grease.

"Tell me." Breed was impatient. "What did you do?"

"Well, sir. I partial cut or filed them trigger main springs. They'd stand up to just plinkin', but to harsh treatment?" He shook his head and frowned. "Hell, they'd snap in a flash. I done the same thing to some of the firin' pins." He laughed. "Filled them cuts with solder. Same results as the springs, I'm sure."

"I'm tellin' you, Gunner," Breed complimented him, "I had two Mexicans shoot at me and neither is alive today. A direct result of your handiwork." Breed dipped his head. "Tell me what you did with the ammo."

"For starters I loaded some hot rounds." Gunner jerked his hand back and snapped his fingers as if he'd just burned them. "And I do mean hot. You could have hit the other end of the plateau from here." He held up a finger for caution. "That is, if the barrel or breech didn't blow up in your face first. Other loads were light. Not 'nuff poop to blow the slug outta the barrel."

"I think I saw a light load–heavy load combination." Breed thought about Blackbeard. "The bolt came straight back. Nasty." Breed grimaced. "Gunner, all I can say is the three of us wouldn't be alive if it weren't for you. Thanks isn't much to say . . ." Breed slapped him on the shoulder.

"My pleasure," he acknowledged. "Someone has to look out for your hide. Now git and let me finish my work."

"See you this afternoon." A wave sent Breed on his way.

"Breed, I'm sorry to bother you, but go over it again. Slowly." General Clemments patiently worked with Breed.

"Sir, if Josie and I can beat Fitz to the bank and strongbox, we can get back the money which rightfully belongs to the United States government." Breed detailed his plan. "Fitz won't expect anyone to be on to his bank account. I have Corporal Calhoun's strongbox key and First Sergeant Alcorn made me a duplicate." Breed handed both keys to the general. "My friend in Deliverance says the bank clerk is new and won't be able to connect names and faces. All we need to do is sign the book and present the keys."

The general vacillated, not convinced of the plan.

"Sir," Breed gently pressured the general. "Time is of utmost importance. If we give Fitz the opportunity, he'll take his money and disappear in a wink. We've got to move quickly."

"What do you think, young lady?" General Clemments looked skeptically at Josie. "Will you help us?"

"General, it should be easy. If only signatures are needed, you could furnish a sample for us." Josie looked confidently at the commanding officer. "I can't see any problems."

General Clemments thumbed through his files and slid a piece of paper across his desk. Josie glanced quickly at it and studied Fitz's and Calhoun's signatures. "General," she volunteered, "I don't think those will be difficult to copy."

"Breed?" The general searched his face for clues and waited for a reply.

"Sir, we have the keys. It's only a matter of getting to the Bank of Deliverance before Fitz does."

"Breed, I normally wouldn't condone this type of behavior, but . . ." The general was lost in thought. "I contacted the territorial judge in Prescott. He's on sick leave and won't return for a damned week." The general spoke in frustration. "My commanding officer, General Longbridge, can't reply for a fortnight. Paperwork, his staff officer told me. Ha!" he scoffed at the weak excuse. "No general is too damned busy to talk to a fellow officer."

"Sir, we have to act quickly," Breed nudged him.

"By damn," the general blurted. "My butt's on the line. Do it!" he snapped. "You with us, Josie?" She consented without hesitation.

"Get going, my dear." General Clemments ushered Josie out of the room. The general spoke with strength of mind to Breed. "I'm concerned about her safety, Breed. Promise you'll look after her."

"I will, sir. Believe me."

"No damned silly chances. Please."

"I'll take No-Feet, sir, if you don't mind. As you well know, he's one hell of a good scout. Besides"—Breed chuckled—"he has a score to settle with Fitz."

The general liked the idea. "You tell him to stick close by. In no uncertain terms!" The general went back to work as Breed left to find No-Feet. General Clemments felt more at ease knowing the Apache was accompanying them.

The ride to Deliverance was hard but not punishing. The worst of the midafternoon heat had risen from the mesa-top and the fresh mounts covered ground rapidly. No-Feet was out front, relaxed on this easy ride. Breed glanced from side to side and occasionally behind.

"You're nervous, why?" Josie inquired.

"I don't doubt for a minute Fitz knows we're coming. For that matter, he might be watching us at this very moment."

"He'd be a fool to hang around here," she boldly stated. A slight pause. "Wouldn't he?"

"With Fitz it's hard to tell. He's managed to stay ahead of all of us 'til now. That's what bothers me."

"How much do you think he has stashed in the bank?"

"It's hard to tell." Breed shrugged his shoulders. "He might have gold, silver, paper. Who knows? For those rifles, both shipments, I would guess around two thousand dollars."

"Whew, that's a lot. What will we do with it?"

"Rightfully it belongs to the United States government. I wouldn't touch it," Breed defiantly announced. "It's dirty money."

"What about Fitz?" Josie wanted to know his fate.

"If he isn't caught soon, I imagine a substantial reward will go up territory-wide. Dead or alive."

"Wouldn't it be something if he were killed by one of those stolen rifles?" Josie shuddered at the thought of Fitz. "I don't think anyone will miss him. We would be better off with him behind bars."

"How about six feet under?"

The lush riverbank shrubs and towering cottonwoods enveloped them with their shady coolness. After the hot ride from Fort Manning, the damp, sweet smell of water enticed them and their horses. Breed's mare was belly-deep in water and he had only to lean over to get a drink. He splashed water over his head and let it run down his back. Deliverance was visible through the trees. A scattered collection of tidy houses skirted the main street and business section of the town. Well-kept hay- and grainfields encircled the town. The community reflected hard work and pride.

Breed left No-Feet at the river and rode into town with Josie. He made arrangements to get together with the Apache and fill him in on their plans after an evening visit to the sheriff's office. As Josie and Breed came into town, she asked him if he had been there before.

"Yes, years ago. I've always liked the place. Good God-fearin' people live here."

"How do they keep it untouched? It's so clean." Josie was enchanted with the looks of the houses and fields that surrounded the town.

"They are mainly Irish and English here. They have their own customs and are willing to fight to keep them. The usual riffraff give this town a wide berth."

"Will Fitz stay away?" She wanted to know what to expect from him.

"No." Breed shook his head. "He has friends here. They'll overlook what he's done."

They trotted down a dusty side street and headed for the corrals behind the stables. Breed laughed and turned to Josie. "Was that your stomach growling or was it mine?"

"I'm famished," she commented, and rubbed her stomach. "Mine's been on the prowl for the last hour."

"I know, I heard it. We'll leave our horses and head straight for the Hotel Ryan." Breed licked his lips. "I'll buy you the best damned dinner in the territory."

The stable boy at Hanrahan's Stables took their horses and told them to hurry to the Hotel Ryan or they would miss dinner. They tramped through the dusty main street and climbed onto the boardwalk of the Hotel Ryan. Breed set Josie's satchel and his saddlebags in the front foyer and together they went straight to the dining room.

After a hearty, home-cooked meal, Breed and Josie lingered over coffee and discussed the last-minute details of tomorrow's bank visit. They had smoothed out the plan as they rode from Fort Manning. "Let's take a walk. I've got to work off some of dinner. We'll walk past the bank and get an idea of the layout." He offered Josie his arm. "Then we'll call on an old friend of mine who might be able to help us with Fitz."

Arm in arm they strolled the length of the boardwalk and window-shopped in the few unshuttered windows. As they passed the bank, they inspected the interior of the building. "Breed, I'm concerned about tomorrow. What if something goes wrong?" Frown lines wrinkled her forehead. "Something we hadn't counted on?"

"What could possibly go wrong?" He sought to calm her. "We've covered every conceivable detail. It'll work"—he patted her hand—"so stop worrying."

They crossed the street and sauntered along the other boardwalk. As they passed in front of the saloon, Breed glanced through the batwing doors. He tensed and stopped walking. Josie clutched his arm. "Let go," he snapped, and jerked his arm free. He turned on his heel and cautiously slipped into the dimly lighted foyer. Josie pressed against the building, afraid to move. Breed futilely scanned the room, then stepped out of the saloon. He came over to Josie.

"What did you see?" Uncertainty was on her face.

"I could have sworn I saw Fitz as we first passed by."

"Could you ask around inside?" she suggested.

"Nope." He pulled her out of the shadows and walked away from the saloon.

"Well, why not?" She was aggravated with him for not answering her more completely.

"Notice the name of this establishment." He nodded over his shoulder.

"Kelly's Shamrock Saloon," she read aloud.

"The local Irish stick together like one big happy

family. Any outsider asking questions is immediately suspect. Besides"—he motioned toward the saloon with his thumb—"inside there are two of the biggest bouncers I've ever seen. I'm not a complete fool, contrary to popular belief."

"What will we do?"

"Let's go visit a friend of mine. He'll know if Fitz is here."

Five minutes later Breed opened the door to the sheriff's office and showed Josie in. A young, gangling lad was seated at the desk and looked up from his book as they entered. The towheaded youth didn't say a word but continued to stare.

"Where are your manners, lad?" Breed asked sharply. "Stand when a lady enters the room."

Breed's words embarrassed the boy. He quickly stood and knocked his chair over backward, which further embarrassed him.

"'Scuse me, ma'am. I didn't mean no disrespect." The boy blushed a light crimson.

"I know you didn't." Josie smiled at him. He's cute, she thought and at that age, awkward and self-conscious.

"Is Jack Kennedy here, son?" Breed searched the room and cells for the sheriff.

"He went to dinner, mister. He should be back right away."

"Do you mind if we wait here?" Breed pulled up a chair for Josie.

"I'll go find him. Pardon me, ma'am." The young man moved toward the door.

"We're in no hurry, lad. Let the man finish his meal." The boy was anxious to leave, but Breed stopped him. It would not be wise to arouse curiosity at the eating establishment. "Go back to your book."

The youth sat and read in silence until muffled footsteps sounded on the boardwalk. Moments later the door opened and Sheriff Jack Kennedy walked in. He was a small, wiry man. Mid-sixties but well preserved. His jet-black hair was combed straight back. Salt-and-pepper sideburns were matched by the same color mustache. His dark skin highlighted Spanish features. He had a confident, slightly aggressive "little man" gait. His dark almond-colored eyes fixed on Josie.

"Howdy, ma'am. How may I help you?"

"I'm with the gentleman there." As she pointed, Jack followed the direction of her finger.

"Breed." A wide grin creased his face. "What a pleasure to see you again." Jack strode quickly to Breed and gave him a warm *abrazo*. Breed returned the greeting. "*Oye, hombre.* You haven't changed much." Jack stepped back and looked at him.

"A little older. No smarter." Breed laughed. "And you?"

"*Mas o menos.*" Jack laughed in return. "Please sit." He motioned both to take a seat. The young boy quickly left the room as Jack waved good-bye to him. Josie hadn't taken her eyes off the sheriff since he entered the room.

"What's bothering you, young lady? I'm not that good looking, am I?" he kidded.

"Oh, I'm sorry." Josie colored. "It's just you're not the Jack Kennedy I had envisioned."

"A long story. Let's say my father was from northern Ireland and my mother from southern Ireland. I mean southern." He spoke in a deep voice, and held his hand at knee height. "Like the pueblo of San Ignacio, Chihuahua. It bothers you, no?"

"No, to the contrary. It's a good combination," she coolly replied.

"*Bueno*. What brings you to Deliverance, Breed? You aren't the social type." Jack got straight to the point.

"I need to know the whereabouts of a certain Irishman named Shamus Fitzpatrick. Former First Sergeant Fitzpatrick. U.S. Army."

"What's he wanted for?" Jack wanted the lowdown.

"You name it and the Army will supply the charges. Murder, kidnapping, gun-running, to name but a few."

"Sounds like an upstanding citizen," Jack commented. "For Boot Hill. When do you need to know?"

"This evening. Is it possible?"

"*Madre de Dios,*" Jack intoned, "short notice. Let me see what I can do." The sheriff stood and saw them out of his office. As Breed turned to shake his hand, Jack added, "I'll drop by your room later this evening."

Breed and Josie went back to the hotel, talked awhile, and went to their respective rooms. An hour later Jack stood in Breed's room.

"You're kidding?" Breed's disbelief was obvious. "You didn't find anything?"

"Using my best Irish connections"—Jack chuckled—"I didn't find a trace. He's probably here but people aren't talking." Jack scratched his head in puzzlement. "I think they are afraid to talk, Breed."

"He's tougher than a hog's nose," Breed warned the sheriff. "Be careful with him."

"*Con calma, hombre.* He's not this tough," Jack spoke as he patted a well-used .45. "I appreciate the warning." Before he let himself out he addressed Breed. "Anything you want me to tell your Indian?"

Breed was momentarily surprised Jack mentioned No-Feet. Then he remembered the sheriff knew everything that happened in the town.

"No, tell him I'll check with him tomorrow. Thanks for your help, Jack."

"*Vaya,*" was Jack's parting word as he closed the door.

The night was one of the longest Breed could remember. He had awakened long before dawn, anxious to set the plan into action, but realized he couldn't roust Josie yet. At seven o'clock Breed could not wait any longer, and knocked softly on her door. No reply. He rapped again, uncomfortable that he might disturb the other guests. After a minute's wait, he paced nervously down the hallway, then returned to listen again. With his ear to Josie's door, two elderly ladies came out of the room next door and gave him disapproving glares.

"Ladies." He politely tipped his hat. They hurried past; neither spoke or looked at him. Breed stepped back and pounded on the door, smarting his knuckles.

"I'm coming. Wait a blessed minute." Josie opened the door a crack. She was angered at the intrusion.

"Mind your tongue, ma'am." He joshed her.

"Oh, it's you. I was asleep," she stated needlessly.

"See you downstairs for breakfast. Fifteen minutes?" He asked impatiently.

"I'll hurry." She smiled at him and closed the door.

Forty-five minutes later Josie drifted into the dining room. She searched for and found Breed in the corner. He stood and held her chair. As she started to sit, he shoved the chair forward to clip her behind the knees. She sat down hard.

"Where in the hell have you been?" he seethed, smiling through clenched teeth.

"I'm sorry. I fell back asleep," she sheepishly confessed. "Someone been spurring you this morning?" she challenged.

"I apologize. I guess I'm a touch jumpy." Breed admitted he was acting like a fool. "This bank deal is grating on my nerves."

The roles were now reversed. Josie took Breed's hand and squeezed it. "Slow down. Let's enjoy breakfast. It will work out. Please?" Her eyes pleaded.

"All right. I'll try and unwind but I don't like this frill and fancy living. I get edgy in the city."

"City?" she teased him. "Remind me never to take you to Kansas City. You'd be in serious trouble."

"I'd rather have a bedroll and the stars than this uppity hotel." As soon as he uttered the words, he regretted his choice of words.

A coy smile creased her lips. "So would I." They laughed together.

The bank teller glanced suspiciously from his caged window as they came through the door. The heavy, glazed-glass-and-oak door closed solidly behind them. The teller was already prejudiced by Breed's uniform. Just another dumb soldier, he steeled himself. He wouldn't speak first, force them to make the first move.

"Mornin'," Breed spoke. "We would like to open our strongbox."

The teller, piqued, spoke down to Breed from his elevated stool. "The strongbox hours are posted on the wall." The man spoke with exaggerated clarity as if he were addressing a child. A love for numbers and busy bookwork suited him to a tee.

"Which wall's them numbers on?" Breed drawled. Two can play this game, he thought.

"Over there. That sheet of paper," the exasperated banker replied.

Josie and Breed walked to the paper and read it with misgivings. The strongbox hours were from 2:30 to 3:30. They would have to wait four and one half hours. Breed felt he was going crazy. He returned to the teller, hoping to sweet-talk him. "About them hours . . ."

"For heaven's sake," the clerk stood and interrupted Breed. "I've never seen . . ." His voice tailed off. The man scurried from behind the cage and hustled to the printed sheet. He underlined each word as he read, "Two-thirty to three-thirty. Right there in plain English. Now, is that all?"

"Yep." Breed was painfully polite, realizing this twit controlled their immediate success. "Thanks fur yur help."

At two-thirty sharp, Breed followed Josie into the bank. The same teller was engrossed in his work. Breed cleared his throat. The clerk looked up; his face fell in resignation. Laboriously he took the keys from his desk and rose.

"What number do you have?" he asked with controlled impatience.

"Here's the key." Breed offered his to the teller.

"Where's the other? I need two."

"You must mean mine," Josie offered. "I completely forgot." She rummaged through her purse, which further annoyed the teller. Josie handed him the key.

"Follow me," he snapped as he led them into the vault.

The strongboxes were tiered ten high by twenty wide. A heavy-gauge steel bar passed through each box handle and secured them in place. The teller's master key opened the bar lock. Breed's key fit one padlock as smoothly as a hand into a silk glove. Josie's key fit but would not turn. The banker fussed with it, then faced Breed.

"This isn't one of our keys," he commented flatly. "It won't turn."

Cold sweat broke out on Breed's forehead. Come on, Gunner, don't let me down. "Please, let me try."

The teller, clearly displeased, stepped back. "Well, if

you think you can do better, by all means go ahead," he goaded Bred.

Breed delicately fit the key into the lock. It turned one third of the way, then caught. He tried to force it. It caught on the same spot. "Fingers are slippery," he excused to the teller.

Breed wiped his hands dry on his pant leg. Casually he grasped the lock and key and muscled it. *Click!* The large lock snapped open. The teller failed to notice the strength Breed had put into forcing the lock. With Breed's help, the clerk pulled the bar through the handles, freeing the boxes.

The tension was physical. Breed smelled his own sour sweat as his armpits dampened. Josie daubed her forehead with a hankie. The clerk pulled at his high, starched collar.

"You'll have to sign the ledger before you can remove the box."

The teller stood beside a small table and opened the ledger. He handed the quill to Josie. She gradually dipped it in the inkwell and glanced down the page. Josie found the signature she sought, Robert E. Lee Calhoun. Calhoun's childlike signature would be easy to match. She held the page flat, underscoring Calhoun's signature with her little finger. With precise strokes she wrote his name. The teller stepped forward, plucked the quill from her hand, and carefully blotted the wet ink. He scrutinized the signature. Satisfied, he turned to Breed and handed him the quill.

Breed approached the table, searched the page but

couldn't find Fitz's signature. He placed the quill below Josie's signature and pressed hard on it. The quill broke. "Damn. Do you have another quill?" Breed turned apologetically to the teller.

The teller, nearly beside himself, walked briskly to the front desk.

"I don't see Fitz's name," Breed spoke softly to Josie. His voice was strained. Josie moved beside him, scanned the page, trying to beat the return of the banker.

"Doesn't matter what name he used. It has to be directly below Calhoun's," she told him. "Look for the same box number, 24-C."

The teller returned carrying a new quill, and with a rapierlike thrust handed it to Breed. As he dipped the point, Breed searched for the name. *Got it!* Shamus Fitzgerald Shaughnessy. Probably his given name, Breed thought. Fitz was smart. Breed labored over his rendition of Fitz's signature. His version wasn't close. A trickle of sweat pooled between his brows. As it traveled down his nose, Breed leaned forward and neatly shook the droplet on the still-wet ink.

"Ah, hell. I need the blotter." He quickly grabbed it from the startled teller and smudged the ink. The name was barely legible.

The nervous clerk stepped in front of Breed and relieved him of both blotter and quill. He studied Breed's attempt at the signature. "That's not the same signature," he said boldly.

"What's the last date we signed in?" Breed countered, assured the clerk didn't know the facts behind the forgery of the signatures.

"You should know. It's your bank account," shot back the teller.

"Roughly twelve days ago," answered Breed.

The man thumbed through the pages and found the last entry. "You are wrong. Exactly two weeks ago. At this very hour, for your information," he added spitefully.

Breed held his fist up menacingly in front of the man, then turned it to show the teller the ugly, pink scar that cut across the back of his hand. The cut was a result of his mad scramble down the logjam on the night Fitz kidnapped Josie.

"My fist met with the front teeth of a horse thief about a week ago. It still pains me when I use it." Breed pulled the humble upbringing routine. "I don't write too good neither." Breed put his finger on the ledger. "That's me." It was a statement of fact. The banker chose not to press the issue.

"Call me when you are finished," he commented on his way to his cage.

Breed removed both locks from the box. Alone at last, he and Josie opened it. Josie couldn't contain her excitement. Breed set half a dozen small leather pouches on the bench and loosened the ties. Three of the pouches contained gold dust, the other three silver. An ornately handcrafted leather pouch contained sixty Mexican gold pieces.

"How much, Breed?" Josie was anxious.

"I don't know but it's a bunch. Fitz has been busy. Look at this." He thumbed through a wrapped packet of hundred-dollar bills. Breed was amazed at the amount of money in the strongbox.

"That's more money than I've ever seen," Josie commented as she gawked at the money.

"You're talking for me also." Breed whistled as he counted one thousand dollars in bills. He opened a manila envelope and laughed. "That man had all angles covered. Confederate bills." Breed marveled at the money. "Fitz had gold, silver, coins, and three types of paper."

"How much would you guess he has here?"

"Maybe three thousand. More than I want to be responsible for."

"It makes me nervous." Josie wrinkled her face and shuddered.

"I wonder how many people died over this." Breed was bitter. "Load your purse," he curtly told Josie.

The strongbox was emptied of its contents. Josie placed half a dozen dirt-filled pouches in the strongbox to give it bulk. She shouldered her weighty purse and walked toward the front of the bank. "Call that mousy bookkeep on your way out. I'll join you in a few minutes."

Together Breed and the teller replaced the box and secured it in place. The teller departed swiftly with his key. As Breed walked past the teller he glanced at the clock. 3:27. He couldn't believe they had been in there that long. A smug confidence settled over Breed. He knew Fitz wouldn't be able to get into the strongbox until tomorrow afternoon.

As they headed for the Hotel Ryan, Breed worried about the late hour. By the time they could check out and get their horses, it would be four-thirty. Too late. He didn't want to risk the ride to Fort Manning in the dark. The decision to stay another night chafed him. If he weren't so concerned with Josie's well-being, he would head out immediately with No-Feet.

"We'll stay the night here and head back to Fort Manning with the early birds. Let's walk by Jack Kennedy's office. He can get in touch with No-Feet and tell him we ride tomorrow morning."

"Will it be safe there?" Josie searched Breed's face for reassurance as he hid the leather pouches and envelope inside the empty water pitcher on the washstand. He draped a towel over the pitcher.

"We don't have a hell of a lot of choices, Josie. Don't worry." He squeezed her hand. "No one will think you have it. Let's go down and enjoy dinner. All that paperwork and waiting made me hungry."

"I hope you're right about the money," Josie added with uncertainty.

After dinner they needed some release from the town, and strolled along the banks of the Sand River. The orange sunset reflected off the gently flowing water. As the sky turned a deep purple, and the evening chilled, they returned to their rooms. Breed's undespairing comments about retrieving the money bolstered Josie but did little to diminish his own feelings of pending disaster. Fitz would strike back. Breed knew it, and made up his mind to stay awake and listen for trouble. With Josie's room next to his, he could hear anything unusual. He pulled his boots off and pushed the rocker to the bed so he could prop his feet up. His .45 rested in his lap.

"Breed, open the door. It's me, Josie."

In a sleepy haze Breed heard Josie's voice calling him. He stood up too quickly. The momentary blackout cleared as he grabbed the chair for support.

"Breed, please open the door," Josie's soft voice called again.

"I'll be there in a second," he whispered. "Let me light the lantern."

Breed walked sleepily to the table. He struck a match with his thumbnail, the flame temporarily blinding him. He lit the wick, lowered the flame, and put the glass chimney back in place. At the door he needed two hands to unlock the latch. Without thinking he stuck his pistol in his waistband, turned the latch, and opened the door.

At the click of the latch, the door exploded inward, smashing Breed squarely in the chest. The combined weights of Cully Kelly and John O'Toole crushed him to the floor. Cully, a svelte 285-pounder, was the local smitty and a tree of a man. He hit Breed waist-high. It was like getting hit with an anvil. O'Toole, a paltry 260 pounds, and the local teamster, drilled Breed in the chest. Breed never had a chance. He was staggered by the door and smothered by 545 pounds of Irish pride. O'Toole knocked Breed as cold as a St. Patrick's day mackerel. Fitz materialized out of the darkened hallway and softly closed the door. He pulled Cully and O'Toole off Breed.

"Damn it all to hell, O'Toole. Now how in the hell can we talk to him?" Fitz prodded Breed with his toe. "He's stiff as a board. Search the room. The loot's here somewhere. Cully, keep an eye on our friend."

Fitz and O'Toole ransacked the room. There weren't many hiding places. They came up empty-handed. "Nothin' here, Fitz. That gal must have it," O'Toole suggested.

"We know it ain't downstairs in the safe. Let's pay the lady a visit." Fitz headed for the door.

Before Cully moved, Breed moaned and stirred slightly. Cully pulled Breed off the floor by his shirt lapels and savagely hit him in the face. Breed was out again. The big Irishman dropped him on his face like a sack of potatoes. "Fitz, me boy, the lad's got a head as hard as yours." Cully rubbed his knuckles and grimaced.

The others laughed along with the clowning of their friend. Out in the hall they talked in muffled voices.

"You two take off," Fitz instructed. "I'll handle the girl."

"Ya, I'll bet you will," snickered Cully. "Oh, Breed," he called in a high falsetto. The three stifled their laughter.

"We'd be more than happy to help," O'Toole volunteered.

"Git the hell outta here." Fitz laughed. "Thanks, boys. I'll square with you later." Fitz playfully cuffed Cully and feinted a jab at O'Toole. The men dodged the blows and slipped silently past him to the hallway exit door.

Fitz waited until they were gone before he tiptoed stealthily to Josie's door. He rapped gently as he whispered. "Josie, It's me, Breed. Let me in."

Fitz put his ear to the door and heard a rustling of sheets. The creaking floorboards told him Josie was coming to the door. The lock clicked and the knob slowly turned. Josie opened the door the width of the safety chain. Fitz lunged forward, hitting the door with his shoulder. The chain snapped. The door caught Josie flush on the nose. She dropped like a rock, clutching her face. Fitz slipped inside the room and closed the door. In the dim light of the flickering wall lantern, Josie looked at Fitz in pain. Terror twisted her face. Blood seeped through her fingers and dripped onto the front of her nightgown. Fitz bent over, grabbed her by the shoulders, and bodily set her on the bed.

"One peep and I'll kill you. Got it?" She moved her head. "Breed's out of working order, so don't bother to call him."

Fitz walked to the nightstand and dipped a cloth in the water basin. Josie's eyes widened. He tossed the damp rag to her. "Put that on your nose. Lie back on the bed and prop your head with the pillow." He snapped out orders.

Josie did as she was told. Fitz's presence terrified her

238

as she remembered back to the night of the kidnapping. He was a ruthless animal. Fitz grabbed a chair and sat beside her. The coolness of the cloth helped ease the pain. Soon she was able to sit, occasionally daubing at her nose. She was intimidated as Fitz leaned closer to her. "I'm going to ask you this only once. Make no mistakes. Where is my money?"

"I don't know . . ." was all she said before Fitz hit her in the face. Pain streaked through her skull as the room light faded. Just before she passed out, the last sounds she heard were a bone-cracking *whack!* and an explosive exhalation of air. She slumped onto the bed at the same time Fitz hit the floor.

Within several minutes Josie came to. The lantern was out but she saw a shadowy figure outlined against the window. The figure slipped through the curtains and disappeared. The soft swish of the fabric was the only reminder of his presence. Josie didn't know what was happening, so she stayed put, afraid to move.

Josie was startled awake by the busy street sounds from outside her window. A quick check of the room satisfied her it was empty. She slid off the bed and went to the nightstand. Before checking the contents of the pitcher, she splashed cold water from the basin on her face. A thorough fingertip inspection revealed that her nose was not broken. The blood on her chin and neck was dried and difficult to scrub off. The beginnings of a beautiful shiner were readily apparent around each eye. With dread she peeked into the pitcher. Empty. She was furious with herself for having let Breed talk her into leaving the money in the pitcher. The hotel's safe would have been the best choice. Josie fought back the sickening feeling Breed was dead. She dressed hastily and left her room.

Josie walked the short distance to Breed's door. She knocked and waited. No answer. She tried the knob, opened the door, and hesitated before entering. Breed was sprawled out on the floor. She rushed over and knelt beside him, but was unwilling to touch him for fear of what she would find. Josie forced herself to rest her hand on Breed's back. He was warm. And breathing. No blood on his back. She would have to turn him over. Using his arm as a lever, she stepped across him and slowly rolled him on his back. Breed moaned and stirred. Josie crossed to the washbasin, got a wet cloth, and wiped his face. Slowly, painfully, Breed sat up and opened his eyes.

"Are you all right?" she asked, not knowing what to expect.

"What happened?" was his shaky answer.

"We had the same visitor last night. I'm still not sure what happened to him." Josie explained her experience.

Breed listened dutifully, then tried to stand. "Help me. I'm still a little light-headed."

Josie struggled against his weight and steadied him as they walked to the nightstand. Breed poured the full contents of the pitcher over his head. He bent forward, submerged his face in the basin, then slowly lifted his head and let the cool water revive him. "Ah, much better. I think I'll live." He took his first shaky steps without Josie's assistance. "I too had a visit from Fitz. He brought along two of his friends." Breed rubbed his chin. "That's the hardest I've ever been hit. They didn't get a thing from me." He shrugged. "I was out cold."

"They must have known all along," Josie commented dejectedly.

Breed shook his head in wonderment. "Fitz has been a step ahead of us, the government, and the law for years."

"The money is gone. You know that?" Josie added.

"I'm not surprised," was Breed's noncommittal answer.

"We've lost all that money and you aren't angry. Why not?" Josie covered her face with her hands and tried to hold back the tears. All their work for nothing. Breed sat next to her and put an arm around her shoulder.

"What more can we do? Fitz is richer and all we have to show are bruises." Breed traced under each of Josie's eyes, and smiled. "We can't chase him. Where would we start. How could we find him?"

"How will we explain this to General Clemments?" Josie was unsure how to approach him.

"Just the way it happened. We've got nothing to be ashamed of. It still gives me a case of the 'red ass,' 'scuse me, to be suckered by Fitz." Breed looked apologetically at Josie. "I look back on his hoodwinking and shudder at my bonehead mistakes."

After an unsuccessful search for No-Feet, Breed left

word with Jack Kennedy to send the Apache back to Fort Manning if he showed up.

Upon their return to Fort Manning, Breed and Josie went directly to the general's office. He received them immediately and got a full accounting. General Clemments patiently listened to both versions. After Josie finished her explanation, a nerve-grating silence quieted the room. The general stood and walked to the window. Following a lengthy pause, he spoke. "I guess we go no further. I don't see what can be accomplished with the man and evidence gone. Do you?" He looked at Breed then Josie.

"No, General," Breed tersely replied. "We'll eat our pride and put the matter to rest. I admit defeat," he added without conviction. Although Josie and the general were surprised to hear Breed close the book on Fitz, they shared his feelings of failure and bitterness.

"If it's of any consolation, Breed, I've blanketed the territory with wanted posters," General Clemments continued. "Fitz will be on the run for the rest of his rotten life. We'll see if we can't bring some Army pressure to bear in this case."

"Good, serves him right. If I were a bounty hunter, he would be my choice." Breed felt better knowing Fitz would be looking over his shoulder for some time to come.

"Let me have your report within the next day or so. One more thing." The general cornered Breed. "Keep me informed on No-Feet. He's too damned good a scout to lose." Breed agreed, but was still mad at the Apache. Where had he been when Breed needed him?

"Josie, I appreciate your help." The general helped her to her feet. "I'm sorry it didn't work as we had hoped. I'm happy to report your father appears well on the road to recovery." The general escorted her to the door. "Take care of him. He needs you."

"Thank you, General." She turned to him and touched his arm. "I regret having failed you." A quick smile graced her. "Now, to go look after Daddy."

The three parted company. They went their separate ways, each feeling they shared a part in the failure of their mission.

CHAPTER
14

The two distant specks moved slowly through the bed of the dry arroyo as they headed for Twin Buttes. Walking Tall's scouts had been following the pair since Blue Pine Mesa. Two braves kindled and flint-lighted a fire for smoke signals to Twin Buttes. Within minutes answering smoke complemented the turquoise sky. One of the riders saw the smoke and figured he and his companion would be dead soon.

Within the hour both men came forward onto the grassy plain between the buttes. The second rider was slightly unsteady as his horse trotted, but his companion dropped back and steadied him. A dozen braves suddenly sealed off the rear. The sides were closed off by a score of Indians. The two men were herded into the center of the plain. One of the outsiders, an Indian, urged his pony forward, pulling the second rider behind him. The man lurched precariously, and grabbed the saddlehorn with both hands, which were bound. The man's shirt was tied over his head, which mercifully blinded him from the imminent danger that confronted him.

Walking Tall and the Indian came face to face, ten feet apart. The single Indian slowly stuck his rifle barrel down between his thigh and the pony. He dropped the tow rope. The two men addressed each other in Apache.

"Why does the ears and eyes of the pony soldiers come here to die?" Walking Tall demanded.

"I have heard on the winds that you wanted the two-tongued gun trader," No-Feet replied boldly. "I bring the gun trader because he is a man of only one heart. A bad heart against our people."

"You have heard well," Walking Tall conceded.

"I have also heard on the tongues of the women that my people say I run from them. I run from no one. Not even you," No-Feet defiantly addressed the chief.

Walking Tall showed no emotion at the insult. "You have a strong pony. He will be needed."

"He runs like the wind on the prairie," countered No-Feet.

Walking Tall looked at his warriors. "My braves have better ponies and can outride you."

"They ride like squaws," No-Feet answered with contempt.

There was a rumbling among the braves. They were insulted and would extract a terrible revenge. Walking Tall turned askew on his pony and pointed up the grassy plain. "When you reach that sage bush, ride."

No-Feet wheeled his pony and trotted to his companion. From his moccasin he pulled his knife and cut the first-sergeant chevrons off the soldier's sleeves. With a backhand flick of his wrist he cut the man's shirt loose from his head. The soldier squinted against the bright sun, closed his eyes, and dropped his head.

The braves let No-Feet pass through their line. After he had passed, they formed a picket line that spread the width of the plain. No-Feet eased his pony into a slow trot and matched himself to its motion. Man and beast were one integral entity. No-Feet reached the sage at a full gallop, yet he viciously whipped the pony. The death race was on. A chorus of war cries and yelps further fueled his desperate flight. Within seconds the sweeping plain was quiet. A soft breeze rustled the deep grass.

The soldier, hands still bound, blinked his eyes and finally cleared them. He hesitantly raised his head to see three Indians staring at him. Walking Tall, Blood, and Spike Buck nudged their ponies forward. First Sergeant Shamus Fitz acknowledged his executioners.

Two weeks after the misadventure in Deliverance, Breed rode point for another infernal wood detail. The

Indians had inexplicably abandoned this sector. Life was relatively peaceful. Movement in the trees caught Breed's attention. He lifted his .45-70 off his lap and headed slowly for the timber. A lone figure on a stubby pony slipped out of the underbrush and rode directly toward him. Breed cradled his rifle when he recognized No-Feet. They stopped alongside each other. No-Feet leaned forward and handed Breed a cloth bundle.

"May your woman give you a son. That is for him." The Apache said nothing more and turned to ride off.

"No-Feet." Breed stopped the Apache's departure. "You'll need this." Breed unbuckled his cartridge belt and handed it to the Indian. A full belt of .45-70 shells was of tremendous value to the Indian. He took the belt and slipped it over his head and shoulder. The Apache heeled his pony in the flanks, rode into the thick under-brush, and disappeared.

Breed looked at the cloth bundle. He slowly unwrapped it and realized he had first-sergeant chevrons in his hands. A small, bone-handled knife of the finest craft had been wrapped in the chevrons. The delicately carved deer-antler handle held a hand-forged and keenly honed blade. This was an exquisite skinning knife. Breed thought about Josie and smiled. He then reflected on the chevrons. Fitz's treachery and greed had no doubt assured him a long and gruesome death. The thoughts of his brutal demise chilled yet pleased Breed. To insult an Indian was dumb, but to double-cross one was sheer stupidity.

"Not a half-bad day after all," Breed told himself. "New marching orders from General Clemments this morning." He smiled with pride about that. "Fitz got what he deserved. And a gift for Josie. Or should I say, for us." He chuckled and rode back to the working soldiers.

The wind swirled around the two massive rock spires of Twin Buttes and scattered the bills like autumn leaves. Reb money and United States currency was strewn about with equality. The sands blew, shifted, and obliterated the gold and silver dust. A returning to the good earth. The gold coin were covered, then lost, under a fine dusting of sand.

Center Point Publishing
600 Brooks Road • PO Box 1
Thorndike ME 04986-0001 USA

(207) 568-3717

US & Canada:
1 800 929-9108
www.centerpointlargeprint.com